Uprising

BY ALEX WHEELER

LUCAS
BooKS

SCHOLASTIC INC.

New York Toronto London Auckland Sydney Mexico City New Delhi Hong Kong

www.starwars.com
www.scholastic.com

ISBN 978-0-545-14086-7

12 11 10 9 8 7 6 5 4 3 2 1   10 11 12 13 14 15/0

Book design by Rick DeMonico
Cover illustrations by Randy Martinez
Printed in the U.S.A.
First printing, May 2010

40

The moon was dead.

A film of red dust lay over the cratered land. Nothing disturbed the still, acrid air. There was no sound; there was no movement. There was only scorched, flat ground stretching to the bare horizon. If life had flourished here once, that time was long over. Erased, all traces of creature or creation wiped out. Gone.

And so there was no one to see the bright star that skimmed across the horizon, nearly invisible in the light of the rising sun.

There was no one to understand that the star was a ship, circling the moon. Its first visitor in millennia.

Certainly there was no one to recognize the ion trail as that of a rusty old CloakShape fighter.

Unseen, the CloakShape orbited the moon, spiraling closer and closer to the thin atmosphere.

And inside, Commander Rezi Soresh — former Imperial Commander, current fugitive — stared blindly into space, and waited to die.

Twenty-seven days, sixteen hours, and four minutes.

That was how long he'd been waiting. Ever since Darth Vader had convinced the Emperor he was a traitor, Rezi Soresh had been on the run.

He snorted. *On the run*. What a joke. *On the crawl* was more like it. Hobbling from one star system to the next. Creeping through the shadows. Desperately scrounging for food, for shelter, for ships. One month before, he had been one of the most powerful men in the galaxy. Then he'd been blamed for the disaster on Belazura — even though it hadn't been *his* mistake that got the Imperial garrison destroyed. The ambush of the Rebels *should* have worked. *Would* have worked, if it hadn't been for the Jedi scum. And even so, it wasn't his fault. Darth Vader had twisted the facts, convinced the Emperor that Soresh was incompetent, maybe even a traitor. All because Vader was jealous of Soresh's power. If Soresh hadn't had a backup escape plan, he would be dead.

But life wasn't worth much anymore. Thanks to the Rebel vermin and the vengeful Dark Lord, Soresh was nothing. Less than nothing.

He was prey.

There were those who believed that the galaxy was teeming with life. Fools. The galaxy was a vast and empty wasteland, small outposts of civilization sprinkled through trillions of kilometers of void. Rezi Soresh was no fool — he knew how to use the emptiness. He knew how to hide.

But Vader was no fool, either, and Soresh had never expected to survive this long. Gradually, as he drifted aimlessly through the wilds of the Outer Rim, something had changed in him. Something had awoken, something he'd never expected to have again: Hope.

Perhaps he was as smart as he'd thought. Perhaps Vader wasn't as powerful as he'd feared. Perhaps he had a chance to save himself, and reclaim his rightful position at the Emperor's side. To get revenge on his enemies.

He had stumbled upon this moon by chance — but perhaps it was destiny.

Soresh dropped altitude and skimmed over the arid land, surveying his new home. It would take time to build a new base of power. It would take resources. But he had ample amounts of both. There were still sources he could risk trusting, secrets he could use to manipulate, to blackmail, to obtain what he needed. As one of the Emperor's most valued advisors, he'd been trusted with a large discretionary fund. Over the years, Soresh had siphoned the money into more than a hundred accounts. He had cultivated a cadre of underlings who would be loyal only to him. He had collected black market information, and knew more about his enemies than they knew about themselves. For one standard month, he had lived as a dead man, afraid to risk any contact with his old life. But living in fear, drifting through nowhere, endlessly *waiting* — it was no better than death. And it was no longer tolerable.

As always, he would be patient, and he would be careful. Soresh knew how his enemies saw him. They thought he was a narrow man, cowardly, paranoid, more comfortable with a datapad than a blaster.

They were right. But they failed to understand that these were not weaknesses; they were his greatest strengths. In the end, they would allow him to rise from the nearly dead. They would allow him to strike back. He would take them all down, all his enemies, all the ones responsible for stranding him here in this brutal no-man's-land.

He didn't have a plan, not yet. But he knew where his revenge would begin. He would start with the one who had started it all, the man who had been the beginning of Soresh's end.

Luke Skywalker.

CHAPTER TWO

Did you say something?" Luke whispered.

"What part of *quiet* don't you understand?" Han Solo hissed.

"I thought I heard my name," Luke said.

"Well, maybe you should *think* a little more quietly," Han snarled.

Chewbacca growled at them.

Luke shut his mouth. When a Wookiee carrying a giant bowcaster shushes you, you take his advice. Especially when he's the only thing standing between you and a roomful of soldiers with blasters.

Luke sighed. Back on Yavin 4, this had sounded like such an easy mission. Go to the Royal Palace of Nyemari, grab the duchess's access codes for the Nyemari Imperial Military Installation, get out. He didn't understand how it had all gone so wrong so fast. Much less how he and Han had ended up crammed into a shoe closet, with only a thin curtain of Dramassian shimmersilk separating them from the duchess's guards. A thin curtain and, of course, Chewbacca, who was posing as a guard himself. Apparently, to most Nyemarians, all Wookiees looked alike.

As usual, Han had been determined to blast his way out of trouble, but Luke and Leia had convinced him to wait. Their orders were to infiltrate — sight unseen. And Leia had insisted they follow orders. Of course, that was before Leia set off to explore the west wing of the palace while Han and Luke took the north and south. She should have rendezvoused with them an hour before, but there was no sign of her. Luke tried not to worry. Leia could take care of herself. Still . . .

"Do you think we should go find her?" Luke whispered.

Han smiled crookedly. "If I know the princess — "

There was a deafening crash and explosion of plaster as a sleek black airspeeder barreled straight through the wall. The room erupted in chaos as guards fled from the oncoming speeder. Laserfire from its forward cannons peppered the room, blasting holes in antique wallpaper, the clari-crystalline vases, and several dozen shoe boxes.

"— she'll find us," Han finished, as he burst out of the shoe closet, blaster blazing.

"What are you waiting for?" Leia cried, urging them into the speeder. White plaster dust coated her braided brown hair.

Luke, Han, and Chewbacca piled in. A phalanx of guards poured into the room. Laserbolts screamed through the air.

"We have to get out of here!" Luke shouted over the noise of battle. He whirled around to send a stream of laserfire at their pursuers. The speeder lifted off the ground.

"Thanks for the brilliant idea!" Leia aimed the speeder straight for the giant transparisteel window. "Duck!"

Luke cradled his head and braced for impact. A shower of transparisteel rained down on them as they hurtled into open air. Two stories below, a fleet of Royal speeder bikes lifted off the ground and gave chase. Leia increased thrust and they shot forward at 650 km/hr.

"I thought you wanted us to do this *quietly*," Han shouted over the engine roar.

"Change of plans." Leia jerked the stolen speeder hard to the right, tipping so precariously they nearly toppled out of the vehicle. She wove skillfully through the maze of skyscrapers, blasting through buildings when she couldn't go around them. The Royal guards were determined, but they couldn't match Leia's piloting skills. "You complaining?"

"Not today," Han teased.

"Feel free to let yourself out," Leia snapped.

Han stretched out in the seat, hands behind his head. "I'm fine right where I am, Your Worship. You can rescue me any day of the week." He coughed loudly, adding under his breath, "Especially when it's your fault we needed rescuing in the first place."

"*Excuse* me?" Leia said.

"I *said* — "

Chewbacca cut Han off with a loud roar. Luke gave the Wookiee a friendly slap on the back. "I'm with Chewbacca," he said. "How about we escape now, argue later?" *Or never*, he added silently. After months of crisscrossing the galaxy with Han and Leia, he was ready for a break.

"In that case, I suggest you hold on." Leia yanked the controls to the right, angling them on a collision course with a thirty-story tower. Luke clung to his seat as Leia pulled back hard. The speeder lurched into a vertical climb, hugging the side of the building. Far below, Imperial speeder bikes skidded and smashed into duracrete as they made clumsy attempts to follow. Leia ignored them. She hunched over the controls, eyes laser-focused on the narrow course ahead of her. There was little for Luke to do but admire her graceful flying as she steered them through the city-sized obstacle course. Their remaining pursuers quickly fell behind, lost in a forest of duracrete and transparisteel.

Soon they were alone in the sky, emerging from the dense city center into an empty stretch of land at the fringe of the capital. The *Millennium Falcon* was parked at a hangar only a few kilometers away.

"Now," Leia said to Han, relaxing her grip on the controls once the danger had passed, "I'd like you to explain *exactly* how this was all my fault."

"You *were* the one who tripped the silent alarm."

"Only because *you* were the one who tripped over your own two feet and knocked me into it."

"Are you calling me clumsy?"

"Of course not! I'm calling you a clumsy, blaster-brained nerf-herder."

Luke sighed and leaned back in his seat. It was going to be a long ride home.

Anem, the capital city of Nyemari, was home to the most modern, architecturally sophisticated spaceport in the Meridian Sector.

Han refused to take the *Millennium Falcon* within a hundred kilometers of it.

Instead, he'd docked the ship at the South Anem Spaceport. It was little more than a large warehouse, built in the no-man's-land where the city bled into the desert. Its equipment and fixtures hadn't been replaced or repaired in three decades. These days, no one bothered to use it but grizzled spacers, smugglers, and any other unsavory characters with shadowy business on Nyemari.

In other words, it was Han's kind of place.

Li Preni, a Nyemarian who'd been fixing up ships at

South Anem Spaceport for years, owed Han a favor. And he'd sworn on his life that he'd take care of the *Millennium Falcon*. But Han didn't trust anyone to take care of his ship — especially not a Nyemarian who'd sell out his own mother for a bottle of lum. The *Falcon* might not look like much, with her crumbling shield projectors and wonky power generators, but treat her right and she'd be your best friend. She was the fastest ship in the galaxy, and Han never felt quite right when she was out of his sight.

But as they approached the main hangar, things felt less right than usual.

It wasn't anything specific. Just a certainty, in his gut, that something was wrong. And Han always trusted his gut — that was why he was still alive. The hairs on the back of his neck stood on their ends. Shadows flickered at the corners of his vision. He swore he heard footsteps behind them, but every time he spun around, the street was clear.

"Calm down," Leia said. "Your precious ship isn't going anywhere."

"What is it, Han?" Luke asked, sounding concerned.

Say what you wanted about the kid and his Jedi hokum, Luke understood gut feelings. But Han shook his head. If he was right, and yet another bounty hunter was on his tail, that wasn't Luke's problem. Luke wasn't the one who'd double-crossed the biggest, ugliest, meanest Hutt this side of the galactic core. Han had been fending off Jabba's minions for months, and he wasn't about to let another one ruin his day.

"Didn't expect to see you back so soon," Li Preni said, as soon as he caught sight of Han. The Nyemarian scurried over, looking shifty and up to no good. But there was nothing unusual about that.

"Didn't expect to see me back at *all*, you mean," Han said. He knew Li Preni wanted the *Falcon* for himself. In fact, Han was half convinced that Preni had been the one to tip off the duchess that they were infiltrating the palace.

"Might have been a better plan," the Nyemarian hissed, leaning in close. Han gagged on Preni's thick, putrid breath. It smelled like a rotting bantha carcass. "Someone's been looking for you."

"Looking for *us*?" Luke said nervously. "Who?"

But Han was unsurprised — his gut was never wrong. "Was it that Farghul bounty hunter slug?" he asked. "You'd think he learned his lesson back on Iridonia."

Preni shook his head. "Just some Glymphid. Offered a big bounty if anyone could point him toward the crew of the *Falcon*."

"And what did you tell him?" Leia asked.

"Told him I never heard of you," Preni said.

Chewbacca growled and took a step closer to the Nyemarian. A big step.

"Okay, okay!" Preni squeaked. "I may have told him

you were in town. But I didn't say you were coming back today, I swear!"

"Only because you didn't know," Han growled.

"Forget him," Leia said. "Let's get out of here before whoever it is comes back."

"Better idea," Han said, drawing his blaster out of its holster. "Let's stick around."

"Han..." Luke tapped the pouch containing the stolen access codes, a reminder that they had more important things to do.

"Don't gimme that look, kid," Han said wearily. They were exactly the same, Luke and Leia, always telling him to *stop*, *think*, *wait*. *Be patient*.

Well, now it was *their* turn to be patient. It was past time to send a message to Jabba. And Han decided this Glymphid was just the guy to deliver it.

eia wanted to throttle Han. As usual. He
was acting like they hadn't just spent three
days on the run. Like there was no rush
to get the access codes off the planet and
back to Yavin 4 — much less get *themselves* off the planet
before the duchess's forces figured out where they were.

How did I get here? Leia asked herself, not for the first
time. Once, the Rebel Alliance had been her only prior-
ity. Destroying the Empire had been all she cared about.
Then, out of nowhere, Luke and Han had dropped into
her life. Destroying the Empire still mattered — but so
did they.

Which was why, fuming, she followed Han out of
the hangar and back into the alleyways of Anem. Good
friends were hard to find — and even harder to ignore
when they were about to do something stupid.

"This way," Han hissed, stepping over a heap of rotting acid-beets. "I think I saw the guy slip around the

corner." Chewbacca's tracking skills and Han's "gut" guided them through the maze of narrow streets. The pavement was cracked and uneven, frequently giving way to rubble. Leia couldn't believe how different this area was from the dense city center, with its glossy, crystalline skyscrapers. There, everything had been smooth and silver. Here, every building was a patchwork of bright colors and mismatched materials. Market stalls dotted each corner, hawking forrolow berries, krayt dragonskin pouches, and small pourstone statues of the duchess. The rich, sweet scent of roasting hambones choked the air. In the city center, speeders jockeyed for space at death-defying speeds. But here, the only traffic was a line of sallow creatures that looked like lumpy, bloated eopie, and the occasional wild pack of roaming voorpaks.

As for the alien they were tailing: More than once, Leia caught a glimpse of a long proboscis or scaled leg disappearing around a corner. But it was always too quick to be caught, too slow to escape them completely. Something was wrong.

But Han wouldn't be stopped. He led them into a cramped alleyway, zigzagging through heaping dumpsters. The heavy stink of rotting garbage was overwhelming. Leia held her breath, walking faster and faster until she was nearly running. She pushed past Han and exploded out of the alley, drawing in a desperate breath of clean air. She nearly choked on it when she spotted the Glymphid standing only a few meters away, his finger extended toward Han.

"Found you!" the Glymphid hissed. The alien was tall and thin, with tan, scaly limbs and suction cups at the end of each narrow finger and toe. Red eyes peered out over a long, sharp snout.

"Worst mistake you ever made," Han drawled. They had landed in a dusty, disused plaza. A decrepit fountain sat in the middle, spigots dry and rusting. They were completely alone with the Glymphid. Leia was suddenly sure that was no accident. "Now, you go back to Jabba and—"

"I have something for you," the alien interrupted, rushing toward them on gangly legs. "Wait!" he yelped, freezing as three blasters and a bowcaster were leveled at him. The alien raised his hands in the air. "It's just a message. I don't even have weapons. You can search me."

"Jabba sent *me* a message?" Han asked.

"Not you," the Glymphid said. "Him." He extended a long, suction-tipped finger toward Luke.

Without thinking, Leia stepped in between Luke and the Glymphid. "What do you want with him?" she asked.

"Him?" Han said, eyes wide. His head swiveled back and forth between Luke and the alien. "You *sure* it's him?"

The Glymphid pulled out a datapad. "The human

traveling with the *Millennium Falcon*, pale hair, low intelligence —"

"Hey!" Luke exclaimed. Han snorted. Leia shoved him.

"— answers to the name of Luke."

"That's you all right, kid," Han said grudgingly.

"I been looking for you for a long time," the Glymphid said. "And it's worth a big reward for me if you just listen to this message." He thrust a holochip and small holo-player in Luke's face.

"What do you think?" Luke asked.

Leia narrowed her eyes at the Glymphid. "We need more information before we can —"

"Let me see that." Han seized the equipment. Before Leia could stop him, he shoved the chip into the player and switched it on.

A shadowy, translucent figure appeared before them, his face masked by a hood. "Luke Skywalker, we finally meet."

"Who is that?" Luke said, staring at the hooded man. He turned to the alien. "Who sent you?"

Taking advantage of their distraction, the Glymphid was creeping away. Han clamped a hand on his shoulder, and dug a blaster into his back. "Not so fast, buddy. How 'bout you stick around while we watch this. Then you're going to answer all our questions."

"I don't know anything," the alien squeaked. "I swear."

"I've been hunting you for a long time," the mysterious figure said. His voice was narrow and pinched. "I believe you know a friend of mine, X-7."

Leia gasped. X-7 had been a skilled assassin hired to kill Luke, and he'd nearly succeeded, more than once. X-7 had been dead for months — but the man who sent him was still out there. Rezi Soresh, the Imperial Commander who'd devoted himself to destroying Luke. Apparently he hadn't given up.

"Meeting you proved rather inconvenient for him," the man continued. "Hopefully, our encounter will end more happily. For me, at least. Now, down to business." He clapped his hands together sharply. His hologram faded into a harsh red landscape of rocks and craters. The camera settled on a group of twenty people, huddled together behind a fence bristling with electric current. Men and women held each other. Small children clung to their mothers' knees. Their faces all bore the same expression: Terror.

"These are some of the passengers of the Arkanian ship *Endeavor*. Settlers — one hundred men, women, and children — headed for a new life on a new world. I'm afraid I forced them to take a slight detour. I'm sure they're eager to get on their way again — and they can. As soon as you deliver yourself to me. At the end of this hol-orecording, you'll find a set of galactic coordinates. You have twelve standard hours to reach them — or I promise you, all my guests will die an extremely painful death. You will *not* tell anyone else about this. If you disobey these instructions, the poor settlers will die." The camera zoomed in on a small child's face, his muddy cheeks streaked with tears. "All of them." The hooded figure wagged a finger at them.

Leia kept her eyes fixed on Luke. She could imagine how he felt. Whenever she closed her eyes at night, she still saw herself on the bridge of the Death Star, watching her beloved Alderaan on the viewscreen. Giving Vader and Governor Tarkin what they wanted hadn't helped, even though she'd told only a half-truth. It hadn't stopped them from proceeding with their "effective demonstra-tion." It hadn't saved Alderaan.

She knew what it meant to have all those lives in your hands, and to be unable to save them. It didn't matter how many people told you it wasn't your fault. It didn't matter if you knew, logically, there was nothing you could have done. If anything happened to those settlers, Luke would never forgive himself.

Leia knew that better than anyone.

"Don't think that you can disobey me just because I'm halfway across the galaxy," the man said. "As of now, I'm watching you. And my reach is further than you might expect. Perhaps you'd appreciate a little demonstration. . . ."

But he didn't move. He didn't do anything.

"Impressive," Han sneered.

And then the Glymphid screamed.

"What did you do to him?" Leia cried.

"Nothing!" Han shouted, as the alien began shaking in Han's grasp. He dropped to the ground, jerking and twitching. His eyes rolled back in his head. Snorts of pain exploded from his snout.

"We have to help him!" Luke exclaimed. He knelt by the alien's side, but there was nothing he could do.

A wracking shudder tore through the Glymphid's body. A long, low sigh wheezed out of his lungs — and then, nothing.

Luke pressed his ear against the alien's still chest, then rose, looking somber. "He's gone."

"Explain to me again what we're doing here?" Lune Divinian said, hoisting a load of duracrete blocks over his shoulder. The Yavin 4 sun was beating down with unusual strength. Sweat matted his shirt to the back of his neck.

"We're offering crucial assistance to the effort to destroy the Empire," Ferus Olin reminded him.

"We're building 'freshers," Div argued. "Not exactly heroic labor."

Ferus lowered himself down to the ground with a soft grunt. "All labor is heroic," he said. But the words rang slightly hollow. His muscles ached with the strain of the heavy lifting. Even his bones ached. It was tempting to call upon the Force to help ease the job along. But they were working on a heavily trafficked path. Anyone could pass by and catch him calling on his old Jedi skills. Ferus couldn't risk it.

"When you suckered me into joining up with this Rebellion, this isn't exactly the kind of work I had in mind," Div complained.

It wasn't what Ferus had in mind, either. After hiding out for two decades, he was eager to *act*. It had been a hard decision to join the Rebellion, as he couldn't risk anything interfering with his primary mission, protecting Leia. But in the end, there was no real choice. If he didn't do everything in his power to destroy the Empire, he wouldn't be able to live with himself. And he knew Div felt the same.

Which didn't mean he'd signed up for refresher building.

"It's going to take them a while to trust us," Ferus said. "Surely you can understand that."

They had both seen what happened when a rebellion trusted too much, too fast. That made it all too easy for enemies to slip under the radar and ruin everything.

"I just don't see how this is helping anyone," Div said. "If we told them what we could do —"

"We can't," Ferus said. "You know that." The Rebels weren't the only ones slow to trust. No one could know that Div had once been a Force-sensitive child, groomed to be a Jedi. As no one could know that Ferus had grown up in the Jedi Temple, training with the great Obi-Wan Kenobi and Yoda himself. "Besides, just because they want to keep us out of the loop doesn't mean we need to let them."

He spied a scruffy redhead making his way through the woods, and flagged him down. Jono Moroni spent most of his time on the Rebel Base doing janitorial work alongside the droids. He was a quiet man who kept to himself, and few people seemed to even notice him. But Ferus's Jedi Masters had long ago taught him the value of silent observers. Jono faded into the background, which meant he saw more than people knew. And he wasn't unwilling to pass it along.

"Good afternoon, Jono," Ferus called out. "How goes it?"

"Couldn't be better," Jono said. Over the last few weeks, Ferus had grown to truly respect the man. He was unfailingly friendly and cheerful. It was clear nothing made him happier than serving the Rebellion. And it turned out that he was only quiet because no one ever bothered to speak to him. Once you got him going, he could talk for hours.

Ferus peppered him with questions about the weather and his recent bout of Balmorra Flu. Gradually, he moved the conversation in the direction he needed it to go. "Things must be busy over at Massassi Station, given what's going on now?" It was a safe question — things were *always* busy at the Rebel Base station.

Jono nodded eagerly. "Course, I shouldn't talk about it."

But Ferus needed him to talk about it. And so he reached out with the Force and loosened Jono's tongue. "You'd like to tell us about it," Ferus suggested pleasantly.

"I'd like to tell you about it," Jono echoed in a fuzzy voice.

Div looked disgusted. It was one thing to use the Force against one's enemies. Using it to wring information from a friend . . . Surely that wasn't the Jedi way. But Ferus wouldn't allow himself to feel guilty. He couldn't help the Rebels unless he knew what help they needed.

Still, such decisions were easier to make in the old days. As a Jedi Padawan it had been simple to know the right thing to do. Right was whatever his Master told him it was. Only after leaving the Temple had Ferus learned the joy of deciding such things for himself. But, like all true joys, it came with a healthy dose of terror. Div knew that, too, in his own way.

"Could be I heard something, while I was mopping up," Jono said hesitantly.

Ferus gave him an encouraging nod.

"Rebel scouts intercepted an encrypted Imperial transmission," Jono confided. "The Imperial High Command is having some kind of top secret meeting in a few weeks, out in the middle of nowhere. Emperor's going. Darth Vader, too. And because they're doing it in secret, they're traveling light. Only a couple Star Destroyers. Sounds like General Dodonna thinks this could be our chance to take down the Empire, all in one shot."

Div scowled. "Great. A top secret mission to take out the Emperor and Vader, and you know where we'll be? Building 'freshers."

Ferus frowned, but for a different reason. "Thank you, Jono. Always good to talk to you. Now it might be nice for you to go back to your quarters and lie down for a bit."

Jono furrowed his brow, looking slightly confused. "Kind of hot out here," he said. "Think I might head back to my quarters and lie down for a bit."

"Sounds like a good idea," Ferus said. *I'm sorry, friend*, he thought, as Jono wended his way through the forest and disappeared into the trees. *You deserve better.*

But he'd learned something — possibly something crucial. "What do you think?" Ferus asked Div.

"I think we're wasting our time out here when we could be —"

"No," Ferus said impatiently. It was growing harder and harder to remember the sweet, young boy Lune Divinian had once been. He'd grown into a hardened, cynical young man. A *good* man — but often, it seemed like he wanted to pretend that goodness didn't exist. Much as he wanted to pretend that his connection to the Force no longer existed. Ferus could understand that. When you'd had great power as a child, only to watch it disappear as you grew, it was tempting to forget you ever had it at all. Ferus had spent many years trying to rebuild his connection to the Force, but he knew he would never regain all he'd lost. "Put aside your impatience and your bitterness. Take a moment. What do you think about what we've just learned? What do you *feel*?"

Div sighed with irritation, but he did as he was told. He closed his eyes and bowed his head. When he looked up, a few moments later, his eyes were bright and clear. "Something's off," he said. "But I can't put my finger on it. That kind of information, just falling into the Rebellion's lap . . . ?"

"I agree," Ferus said. "It's almost too easy."

"We are due for some good luck," Div pointed out.

"Not likely," Ferus mused. It would be nice to believe that the galaxy had finally smiled upon the Rebellion. But doubt gnawed at him. Something felt very wrong about this news. A great pressure seemed to weigh down on him, as if the dark side was settling on Yavin 4, thickening the air, spreading its poison.

"Maybe it's time for us to get out," Div said. "You think something bad's coming, I can tell — seems like a good time to get out, while the getting's good. Go save the galaxy from somewhere else."

"You don't mean that," Ferus said.

Div opened his mouth — but shut it again, before arguing.

"We've got some time," Ferus said. "We can figure this out."

"And if it's a trap?"

"Then we do whatever we have to do to keep the Rebels from flying straight into it," Ferus said, hoping he sounded more confident than he felt. He told himself there was no reason for the dark chasm of hopelessness that had opened within him.

At least the princess is far away from here, Ferus reassured himself. *Whatever happens, she'll be safe.*

Han, Luke, Leia, and Chewbacca gaped at the dead Glymphid.

Luke cleared his throat nervously. "You don't think . . . I mean, there's no way a holorecording could . . ."

"Coincidence," Han said, watching the holoplayer like it was going to bite him. "Had to be."

Chewbacca growled in agreement.

"I've heard of delayed-release poisons," Leia said. "Maybe activating the holoplayer triggered something?"

"Maybe we should leave before it triggers something *else*," Han suggested.

Luke stared at the coordinates that the hooded man had given them. "This is halfway across the galaxy," he said. "Even if we leave right now, we might not make it there in time."

"That's assuming we go at all," Han said. "You want to walk straight into a trap?"

"I'm not going to just leave those people to die!" Luke said indignantly.

"And I'm not looking to die with them," Han shot back. "Self-sacrifice isn't in my vocabulary, kid."

"Then I'll go without you," Luke said.

"Oh, yeah?" Han grinned. "In what ship?"

Luke glared at him, furious. Whenever he let himself believe that Han cared about anyone but himself, something like this would happen.

"Let's slow down," Leia said. "We should contact the Rebel base, let them know what happened, see what they —"

"No!" Luke exclaimed. "Didn't you hear Soresh? If we disobey him and tell anyone what's happening —"

"It's a bluff, kid," Han said. "No one's watching."

"How do *you* know?" Luke asked. He glanced at the dead alien. "I bet *he* didn't think anyone was watching, either. And now look at him. I'm not going to let anyone else die because of me."

"This is *not* your fault," Leia insisted. "And if anything happens to those hostages, that's not your fault, either. You can't control what some maniac decided to do."

"Maybe I can't control it," Luke agreed. "But I can stop it. And I'm going to." None of them understood, maybe because it hadn't been *their* name on the holovid. This was all happening because of him. Because for whatever reason, this insane Imperial wanted Luke Skywalker, and was willing to kill. *Enough people have died to protect me*, Luke thought. Images of his aunt's and uncle's smoldering bodies, of Darth Vader's lightsaber slicing through Obi-Wan Kenobi, flashed through his mind.

Enough.

"Fine," Leia said. "But you're not doing it alone."

Chewbacca hooted with enthusiasm. He was always eager for battle. Which left only one.

Leia fixed Han with a steely glare. Stubbornly, he met her gaze. Then he sighed.

"Your wish is my command, Princess," Han said wearily. "But if we do this, we do it my way. We're not just delivering the kid up to the slaughter. We've got to be smart."

"Smart?" Leia raised her eyebrows. "I thought you said you wanted to do this your way."

Han lowered the *Millennium Falcon* into the atmosphere, surveying the moon's features.

There weren't any.

People talked about "the middle of nowhere," but Han realized that he'd never actually been there — until now. Soresh's coordinates had led them to the Sixela system, a forgotten wasteland deep in the Outer Rim. The moon of the third planet around the blue giant star was habitable but uninhabited, and Han could see why. There was nothing on the ground but rocks and dust. The instruments indicated only one concentration of life, a small outpost at the moon's equator. Han projected the image on the viewscreen. It was a cluster of small, fortresslike buildings surrounded by the electrified pens they'd seen on the holovid. Large laser cannon installations surrounded the pens, aimed at the prisoners. But there was no indication of any other weapons systems or planetary defense.

Han grinned. Whoever this Soresh was, he clearly didn't know how to lay an ambush. This was going to be a piece of puff cake.

"Pardon me, Captain Solo?" Luke's golden protocol droid walked stiffly into the cockpit. His astromech counterpart wheeled in beside him "Are you absolutely sure you wish to take such a rash course of action?" C-3PO asked, for the hundredth time. "Perhaps if you would let me negotiate with the Imperial Commander? After all, I am a protocol droid, well versed in forty-seven forms of hostage negotiation —"

"You don't negotiate when someone's got a blaster to your head," Han said impatiently. "You use a bigger blaster."

The astromech droid, R2-D2, beeped and whirred.

"Yes, Artoo, I'm sure Captain Solo *does* know what he's doing. I simply wanted —"

R2-D2 issued a high whistle.

"Oh, really?" C-3PO said. "And when exactly is the last time *you* used a blaster?"

The astromech droid beeped a response.

"I most certainly will *not*," C-3PO said huffily. "Why don't *you* jam a restraining bolt in your —"

"Enough!" Han shouted. "I can't think with you two yammering in my ear."

"Certainly, Captain Solo," C-3PO said, offended but obsequious. "We'll leave it to you."

"Good," Han growled. He prepared the ship for landing. The laser cannons were armed and ready, and his blaster, as always, was by his side. "I've got some negotiating to do."

Han set the *Falcon* down on the moon, about half a klick from the hostages. A solitary figure stood in the red sand, waiting.

"Stay here and stay out of trouble," Han instructed the droids. Then he and Chewbacca disembarked. The air was thin and choked with dust, but breathable. The man standing before him wore a hood over his face and carried an ancient triple blaster. It hung loosely at his side.

"Greetings, Captain Solo," he said. "Welcome to my kingdom."

"So you're Soresh?" Han said.

The man nodded. He took a few steps toward the *Falcon*.

Han raised his own blaster and aimed it toward the Imperial. "How about you stay where you are and I stay where I am until this is settled," he suggested.

"I have no argument with you," Soresh said. "I trust you've brought Luke."

"I have," Han said. His finger tensed on the blaster trigger. He was the one who had come up with this plan — but that didn't mean he was sure it would work. Not that he would ever admit as much out loud.

"And where might he be?" Soresh asked, in a pinched voice.

"He might be inside the ship," Han allowed. As he spoke, an X-wing fighter roared into the atmosphere, laser cannons blazing. Right on time. Han grinned. "Then again, he might not."

A second X-wing followed on the tail of the first. They spiraled through the air, strafing the weapons embankments with carefully aimed bursts of laserfire. One after the other, the cannons exploded. The hostages cheered.

"You don't realize what you've done," Soresh said, raising his blaster.

But, distracted by the surprise attack, he moved too slowly. Han fired first, and his aim was true. Soresh flew backward, scorch marks spreading across his chest. The Imperial's shot went wild, sending a harmless burst of laserfire into the sky. He landed several meters away, kicking up a cloud of red dust. Han approached the body, blaster at the ready, but Soresh didn't move. His eyes gazed sightlessly up at the sky; his chest lay perfectly still. He was dead.

It was over.

Luke couldn't believe everything had gone so smoothly. By all reports, Commander Rezi Soresh was some kind of strategic genius — but apparently his skills were overrated. Because there was Soresh, lying on the ground dead, his plans destroyed in under five minutes.

He landed his X-wing beside Leia's. She was grinning.

"I can't believe that actually worked," she said, climbing out of the starfighter.

"What was that about my genius plan?" Han joined them, looking incredibly proud of himself. "I didn't quite hear you."

Leia ignored him. "Let's just worry about the hostages," she said, "so we can all go back to normal."

"I'll get Artoo," Luke suggested. "I bet he'll be able to figure out how to turn off the electricity and release them."

He flipped opened his comlink to summon the droid.

"I don't need some tin can to tell me how to flip a switch," Han said, heading for the prisoners' pens. "I'll just — ahh!"

The earth exploded beneath his feet. He flew backward, landing with a hard thud. Luke and Leia ran toward him, as the explosions continued. The ground beneath the prisoners' pens lurched and buckled, as if wracked by a series of massive groundquakes. *Or underground mines*, Luke realized with horror. Chaos erupted, and there was nothing he could do to stop it. Hostages screamed as they were thrown through the air by explosion after explosion. The electrified field failed, and prisoners fled across the red dust, terrified and bloody. Surrounded by wounded, desperate survivors, Luke lost sight of his friends. All he could see were the faces of frightened strangers, begging for his help.

One of them, a slim man with a pale, narrow face, limped toward Luke. Blood trickled from a wound in his forehead and flowed freely from a gash in his right leg. "Please," he whispered. "Help us."

"I will," Luke promised, hoping he could follow through.

The man threw his arms around Luke in gratitude.

"It's going to be okay," Luke said quietly.

"It will now," the man said. "Now that you're here. *Luke*."

Alarm shot through Luke. He reached automatically for his lightsaber. But his hand had barely closed over the hilt when a force pike suddenly materialized in the man's hand. It slashed through the air, landing hard on

Luke's back. A concentrated nerve impulse shot through his body. As Luke's limbs went completely numb, his legs gave out beneath him. The man lowered him gently to the ground.

"Soresh . . ." Luke croaked as his throat closed up, choking off his words.

"A pleasure to meet you," Soresh said.

Luke tried to stand. He tried to reach for his lightsaber. He tried to call out, to warn his friends, to do anything. But all he could do was lie still as screams ripped the air. Darkness crept up on the corners of his vision, blotting everything out. Luke battled to stay conscious, but the force pike had overwhelmed his nervous system. The last thing he saw was Soresh's ghoulish smile.

And then the darkness won.

CHAPTER FIVE

Luke opened his eyes. He found himself lying in a dark cell. Stun cuffs wrapped around each wrist were attached to the wall by thick chains. He was trapped.

Every muscle in his body screamed in pain, and when he tried to rise on his knees, his legs wobbled beneath him. The blow from the force pike had left him too weak to stand, nearly too weak to move. He knew the effects would wear off . . . but then what? Once he got his strength back, he was still chained to a wall. And even if he could escape his bonds, thick durasteel bars stood between him and freedom.

Luke reached for his lightsaber — its blade could slice through durasteel like it was bantha butter. But the lightsaber was gone.

He sagged back to the ground, hope fading away. A true Jedi never let his lightsaber out of his sight. But Luke had never felt less like a Jedi in his life. He had failed.

Failed at rescuing the prisoners, failed at warning his friends, failed at saving himself. He should never have tried to trick Soresh. Who knew how many hostages had died because of his pride?

"Well, well, well," a familiar voice said. "So this is the famous Luke Skywalker, the man who destroyed the Death Star, who bested my best assassin. I have to admit, I thought you'd be taller."

Luke used all the strength he had to drag himself off the ground and meet Soresh eye to eye. The chains were just long enough to allow him to stand. But they kept him pinned to the wall, preventing him from crossing the cell and wrapping his hands around Soresh's throat.

"Where am I?" Luke said, trying not to sound afraid. "Where are my friends?"

Soresh clucked his tongue. "I suspect you'd rather not know their fate."

"What did you do to them?" Luke shouted. A wave of anguish swept over him. He had to escape. If Leia and Han were in trouble, he had to do something. If anything happened to them, just because they'd insisted on sticking by his side . . .

"I'm the one you want," Luke said. "You made that clear. Let them go, and do whatever you want to me."

"I can do whatever I want to you anyway," Soresh said coolly. "So I see no reason to bargain. And, as I say, your friends' fate is already sealed. As is yours."

Luke struggled against the cuffs, lunging toward Soresh, but the chains held fast.

"Just be patient," Soresh advised. "We'll begin soon, and then all will become clear to you." He turned his back on Luke, and began walking away into murky darkness.

"Begin what?" Luke shouted.

No answer came. He would have to do this on his own. Somehow.

Concentrate, Luke thought. He had done this before, and he *knew* he could do it again. But summoning the Force meant clearing his mind, turning within, *focusing*, and that was nearly impossible. He was too desperate, too worried about Leia, Han, Chewbacca, and all the prisoners. He knew that he had to stop trying so hard — that accessing the Force meant letting go. But the harder he tried to stop trying, the more useless it was.

Forget everything else, he thought, trying to pretend that Ben was there beside him, urging him on. *Just focus on the stun cuffs.*

He gazed intently at the cuffs, taking in their shimmering black surface and the smooth curve of the durasteel. He closed his eyes for a moment, concentrating on the cool pressure around his wrists. He imagined he could see inside the cuffs, to the molecules strung together, chaining him in his prison. The Force flowed through those cuffs, as it flowed through everything.

And if he could connect with the Force, maybe he could encourage those molecules to expand. Just a little, just enough to slip his arms free. *Help me out*, he begged the stun cuffs, feeling slightly ridiculous. *Let me go.*

Luke didn't know how long he sat motionless, concentrating on the cuffs, trying to break their bonds. It felt like hours; it could have been minutes. And then it happened. Like a switch had flipped, deep within him, he knew: If he tried to pull his hands out of the cuffs, they would give.

"Please," he whispered. Then wrapped his right hand around the cuff on his left wrist, and pulled.

The cuff slipped down his wrist, over his hand, and got caught on his knuckles. He tugged harder, wincing as his bones crunched together. His hand was slippery with sweat, but he refused to give up. *Just a little wider*, he thought, trying to feel the Force flowing through the cuff, through his wrist, helping him to freedom. He gave one final, mighty tug—and the cuff slipped off. The other slid over his right hand effortlessly. He was free!

Free, that is, if you ignored the thick durasteel bars trapping him in the cell.

Luke sighed with relief, rubbing his sore wrists. His hope was returning. If he could use the Force to expand the stun cuffs, then couldn't he do the same thing to the durasteel bars? If he could widen them by only a few inches, he could slip right through.

He wrapped his hands around the bars — and screamed.

An electric shock sizzled through his body. He flew backward, slamming hard into the floor. His head clanged against the durasteel. He nearly blacked out with the impact. Waves of pain crashed over him, but Luke struggled to stay afloat — and awake. His mind was muddy, confused, and everything was blurry. He blinked hard, trying to clear his vision. Trying to *think*.

The bars must have been electrified, he thought.

That explained what he was doing on the floor.

But it didn't explain why he couldn't get up. It wasn't like the impact of the force pike. His limbs weren't paralyzed. They were just extremely heavy, like a giant weight pinned him to the ground. It took all the effort he could muster just to keep breathing. And he wasn't sure how long he'd be able to manage that.

Luke had never felt so frustrated. What good was the Force at a time like this? Jedi were supposed to be all-powerful — but it was becoming more and more obvious to him that he was no Jedi. Perhaps Obi-Wan Kenobi would know what to do. But Ben was dead. All the Jedi were dead. Which meant it didn't matter how much power Luke had — without anyone to show him how to use it, he was weak. And completely powerless.

Footsteps approached the cell, and he heard the sound of slow applause. It took all the strength he had just to turn his head. Soresh grinned down at him.

"Not bad," Soresh said. "Just not good enough. But we'll fix that."

Luke opened his mouth and tried to speak, but the crushing pressure on his lungs was too much. He managed little more than a pathetic gasp.

"Surely you can understand that before we got started, I had to see how much control you had over the Force," Soresh said, as if Luke had spoken. "Oh, you're surprised I know about your little Jedi secret? You have no secrets from me. You'll learn that soon enough."

Luke gasped again. His chest barely rose with each shallow breath. The lack of oxygen was making him dizzy.

"Oh, let me help you," Soresh said. He reached toward the wall, fiddling with something Luke couldn't see. Abruptly, the pressure released. Luke drew in a deep, grateful breath. "Perhaps I should have warned you," Soresh added. "There's an electromagnet beneath the floor, and you've been injected with a ferromagnetic solution. All I need to do is activate the magnet and . . . well, you see what happens. So now you understand there's no need to waste your energy trying to escape."

"What am I doing here?" Luke asked, when his lungs had recovered enough for speech. "What do you want?"

"You took away one of my most valuable possessions," Soresh said. "I believe you knew him as Tobin Elad."

"X-7," Luke said. "Your assassin."

"My former assassin," Soresh said. "He's not much use to me as a corpse."

"I didn't kill him," Luke said.

"Maybe you didn't strike the final blow, but he's dead because of you. And now you're going to pay for your crime." Soresh stepped away from the cell for a moment and returned with a narrow tray of food. He slipped it through the bars. "I suggest you eat it all," he said. "You'll need your strength."

Luke's stomach turned at the sight of the nerfsteak. "Why bother," he spit out, refusing to let Soresh see his fear. "If you're just going to kill me anyway, why waste your food?"

Soresh laughed. It was a hard, twisted sound, like a wounded fynock. "You've misunderstood me, Luke. I'm not going to kill you — I'm going to make you great."

"What are you talking about?" Luke asked. He had confronted many evil men over the last few months. He had learned to be brave in the face of darkness. But there was something different in Soresh's gaze, something beyond evil. They were the eyes of a man trapped in a nightmare. And now Luke was trapped there with him.

"You killed X-7," Soresh said, a crazed smile fixed on his skeletal face. "So now you're going to replace him."

"Who are you?" Leia shouted, as the men tossed her into a cell. They wore identical black uniforms. Although the guards were different heights, colors, builds—different in every way—there was a strange *sameness* about them. But Leia couldn't figure out why. "Why are you doing this? Do you know who I am?"

"Do you know who *I* am?" Han said loudly, speaking over her. He shot her a pointed look, and Leia had to admit he was right. If they didn't know who she was, it was probably better they stay ignorant.

"I'm the guy who's gonna blast all those holes through you," Han answered his own question. Though, given the fact that they'd stripped him of his weapons, it was an empty threat.

Chewbacca had taken down six or seven of them before they captured him, but even the Wookiee couldn't fight forever. He was shoved into the bare cell with his two friends.

The men, whoever they were, never looked their prisoners in the eye. They never spoke, not even to one another. Leia had managed to knee one in the gut, but he hadn't grunted in pain. He had barely even flinched, and the blank expression on his face never changed. It was like they were droids. It was like they were empty.

"Don't you dare leave us in here," Leia ordered, as they slammed and locked the cell gate.

One of the men finally did look up and, perhaps accidentally, caught Leia's eye. She shivered. There was something . . . *wrong* about his gaze. Something empty.

And then the man was gone.

Leia tried to shake off the horror. "This is all your fault," she muttered. When in doubt, arguing with Han always seemed like the best course of action. You could usually count on him to be wrong. But mostly, she just wanted some noise to fill up the silence in the cell. And to drown out her thoughts. There was an idea bubbling up in her, an idea she couldn't tolerate. Fighting with Han was the perfect way to ignore it.

"My fault?" Han echoed. *"My fault?"*

"Yes, your fault!" Leia said. She sat with her back against the wall of the bare cell. Han prowled the other side, searching for cracks in the wall. Chewbacca wrapped his giant paws around the durasteel bars, trying to pry them apart. But it was no use. The Wookiee roared in frustration. "See?" Leia said triumphantly. "Even Chewie thinks it's your fault."

"You going to listen to that furry oaf?"

Chewbacca growled, sounding insulted.

"Sorry, buddy," Han said quickly. "But Her Royalness here knows that if anything, this is *her* fault."

"*My* fault?" Leia repeated.

"You got it, sweetheart. If you hadn't landed so quickly—"

"If you hadn't *shot* our only leverage—"

"Oh, yeah? Well, if you hadn't . . . if *you* hadn't . . ."

"Where do you think they took Luke?" Leia asked quietly. She couldn't ignore it any longer.

"I don't know," Han said. "But you know the kid. He can take care of himself. Probably fought 'em off with some of that Jedi magic of his." He didn't sound convinced.

Leia didn't say anything.

"Hey, don't worry," Han said awkwardly. "We're all going to be fine."

She had to smile. It was always a little entertaining whenever Han tried to be sincere. He was so . . . *bad* at it.

"We've gotten out of tighter jams than this one," he reminded her. "About a thousand of them."

"I know," Leia said. "You're right."

But she couldn't stop seeing the look in those men's eyes, empty and soulless. And she couldn't ignore the truth any longer. She remembered where she'd seen a look like that before: X-7, the brainwashed assassin. He'd been brainwashed by Soresh, the Imperial who had trapped them here. And Leia was starting to think that Soresh had built himself a soulless, empty-minded army.

That was bad enough, but not as terrifying as the obvious question: How many more soldiers did he need?

"I simply was not built for this kind of situation!" C-3PO exclaimed, crouching stiffly behind a large red boulder.

R2-D2 beeped sadly.

"Yes," C-3PO agreed. "You'd think I would be used to it by now."

The protocol droid and his astromech counterpart had watched their friends being dragged away to some kind of underground fortress. Now they were alone on the surface of the moon. And they had no idea what to do next.

The astromech droid was rolling in slow circles, his neural circuitry whirring with furious thought. Suddenly he released a shrill whistle.

"Oh, we have to help them, do we?" C-3PO said, sounding irritated. "That's all well and good. But how exactly do you expect us to do that?"

R2-D2 trilled a speedy response.

"Me? You want to know if *I* have an idea?" C-3PO said.

R2-D2 beeped a yes.

"My idea is that we go back to the ship and stay out of trouble, just like we were told," C-3PO said. "I'm sure Master Luke and the others are perfectly capable of saving themselves."

The astromech droid stopped in his tracks, and unleashed an angry burst of beeps and whistles.

When he finished, C-3PO leaned stiffly against the boulder, defeated. "Yes, I know Master Luke would do the same for us," he admitted. "But how are we supposed to help?"

R2-D2 extended his manipulator arm and began drawing an outline in the red sand, beeping with excitement.

"*You* have a plan?" C-3PO cut in. "Well, why didn't you just say that in the first place?"

The astromech droid beeped.

"Since when do you care about being polite?" the protocol droid exclaimed. He threw his arms in the air. "All right, let's hear it."

R2-D2 laid out his plan. C-3PO calculated a one in 2,341,900 chance of success.

They immediately got to work.

• • •

Ferus perched awkwardly on the narrow stool, waiting for General Dodonna to finish the mission briefing. Rows and rows of pilots sat stiffly at attention. They were all eager to hear about their new mission. Under any other circumstances, Ferus would be thrilled to join their ranks. It meant Dodonna finally trusted him and Div. Or at least, trusted them enough to let them join the Rebels for this mission. The general was sending nearly half the fleet. Normally, a mission briefing would be delivered shortly before the ships set out. But this time, General Dodonna was giving his fighters two weeks to prepare and train. Even if the intel was right, and there would only be two Star Destroyers guarding the secret Imperial meeting, Dodonna was taking no chances.

"We will launch the ambush from these five strike points," General Dodonna announced, diagramming the attack on a large screen. He went on to explain the complicated maneuvers and split-second timing the mission demanded. The fleet was going to need practice. "And if this effort succeeds, it may be the end of our long and difficult fight," he exclaimed. "A new day is dawning!" The room erupted into cheers.

As the crowd of Rebels dispersed, Ferus made his way to the front of the room. "General, might I have a word with you?" he asked. Though they had met before only briefly, the general had a reputation for being generous with his time. He was willing to hear anyone out—especially anyone who was a friend of Princess Leia's.

"Walk with me," the general suggested. He was older than Ferus, but there was something youthful about him. A certain energy and optimism that Ferus had lost long ago. However old he was, he was still young enough to hope.

They descended a turbolift together and exited the building. "I've grown quite fond of this moon," General Dodonna mused, as they strolled through the forest of dense Massassi trees. "It's a shame we'll have to evacuate soon." Then he smiled. "Of course, if this mission works, perhaps we won't have to."

"That's actually what I wanted to speak with you about, General," Ferus said. Then he hesitated. He had spent two decades on Alderaan, cozying up to powerful men of the court. But that had been when he was pretending to be someone else—someone with no character and nothing to say. Ferus had learned to hide in plain sight, acting as a mirror for whatever pompous stuffed shirt he was trying to impress. All so he could protect the princess—and it had worked. But it hadn't taught him anything about how to argue his point gracefully. In fact, it had been far too long since he'd had to speak up for himself with a stranger, to be honest about what *he* believed. So he did it fast, like ripping off a patch of synthflesh. "I'm worried about this mission. Something's not right."

The general stopped walking. "What do you mean?"

"It's just a gut instinct," Ferus said. "But I fear it's a trap."

"We received this intel from an extremely trusted source who would rather die than betray the Alliance," Dodonna said. "Do you have evidence we should distrust his word?"

"No . . ."

"And is there some reason I should let the fate of the Rebel Alliance rest on your *instinct*?"

For a split second, Ferus considered telling the general the truth. But he feared that it wouldn't do much to help his case. Even a Jedi instinct was still an instinct. It wasn't proof. "Maybe if you let me take a look at the Imperial transmission," Ferus suggested. "I was quite the slicer in my day, and I could probably . . ." He trailed off. General Dodonna was shaking his head.

"I like you, Ferus," the general said. "But I have no reason to trust you with classified material. The only reason you've even been allowed this much access is that Princess Leia vouched for you."

"Then perhaps we should contact the princess," Ferus said quickly.

General Dodonna tensed. It was a nearly imperceptible tightening of the muscles around his eyes and mouth.

Most people would never have noticed. But Ferus wasn't most people.

"What is it?" Ferus asked urgently. "What's wrong with the princess?"

"Nothing," the general said, too quickly. "As you know, she's on a covert mission, and can't be reached."

"Her covert mission ended three days ago," Ferus said. He kept very careful track of Leia's whereabouts. "She's supposed to be on a diplomatic visit to the Winagrew system."

General Dodonna rubbed his temples. "I suppose there's no harm in telling you. . . . Princess Leia and her team have been out of contact since leaving Nyemari."

Ferus drew in a deep breath, forcing himself to calm down. The idea of Leia in danger caused him a nearly physical pain. And it wasn't just Leia, either. Luke was with her. The galaxy's two best hopes for survival . . . lost somewhere in the emptiness of space.

"There's no cause for alarm yet," the general said, sounding rather alarmed himself. "We're doing everything we can to locate them. And it's entirely possible the *Millennium Falcon*'s communications instruments are malfunctioning. Just like everything else on the ship."

Possible . . . but not likely. Leia would never allow herself to be out of contact with the Rebellion for this long. Not unless she had no other choice.

• • •

"Help!" Leia screamed. Han lay on the ground, gasping and shuddering. "I don't know what's wrong with him, he needs a medcenter! Please, help us!"

Chewbacca's roars echoed against the duracrete walls. Leia knelt by Han's body, shrieking louder and louder. Finally, help arrived. Two men appeared at the gate of the cell. One had a bushy brown beard, the other was bald. Both carried blasters. "Quiet," one of them said, in a dull, empty voice.

"You have to help him," Leia said. Tears streamed down her face. "He just collapsed. I don't know what happened. Please."

The men unlocked the gate of the cell and swung it open. As soon as they did, Chewbacca lunged for their blasters. Han sprung to his feet, grabbing the nearest guard around his knees and throwing him to the ground. The guard rolled over, struggling to reach his blaster, but Han kept him pinned. Out of the corner of his eye, he could see Chewbacca twisting his prey into a knot. Han slammed a fist into the guard's stomach, then delivered a blow with his forehead. The guard barely reacted to the pain. Nor did he stop fighting. The blaster lay on the ground, only a few meters away, but every time Han lunged for it, the guard's swinging fists knocked him away. It wasn't just that he was especially strong or especially fast—though he was both. It was the way nothing distracted him from his goal, from

Han. Han was starting to get the feeling this guy would fight to the death. And that he wouldn't particularly care whose death it was.

But Han *did* care, and maybe that finally gave him the advantage. He gave the guard a mighty heave, sending him thumping to the ground, then lunged for the blaster. His fingers grasped the butt of the weapon. Almost simultaneously, he yanked the guard off his feet and pressed the blaster to his head.

"Han!" Leia screamed.

Han looked up. Three new guards had appeared in the doorway, and one of them pinned Leia with her arms behind her back.

"Let her go!" Han shouted. He had his arm locked around the neck of the bearded guard. His other arm held a blaster to the man's head. Chewbacca held the other guard by the nape of the neck, dangling him several inches off the ground. "Let her go or we'll let your friends have it."

"You're ordered to behave," one of the newly arrived guards said. He raised a blaster.

"I mean it," Han shouted. "I'm not bluffing. I'll shoot."

A bolt of laserfire shot from the guard's blaster — and smashed straight into Han's. The weapon flew out of his hands, sizzling with the impact. Then the same guard fired another shot. It slammed into the bearded guard's chest.

Han was stunned. "You shot your own man."

"He failed," the guard said simply. He raised his blaster again, but Han put his hands in the air. After a moment, Chewbacca did, too, releasing the bald guard. The man didn't run away from the Wookiee. He didn't even move. It was as if he expected to be shot, too — and was just waiting for it.

"You may go," the guard at the door told him.

Without any visible sign of relief, the bald man walked out of the cell. The other guards shoved Leia back inside, then locked the cell again and disappeared without another word.

"Great plan," Leia said, slumping against the wall.

"Hey, it should've worked," Han complained. "How was I supposed to know they'd be like . . . *that*. It's not natural."

Chewbacca growled in agreement.

"You're right," Leia said gloomily. "It's not."

They sat in silence for a long time. Han refused to give up, but he had to admit, he was out of ideas — and it seemed like everyone else was, too.

"Don't try that again." A man appeared at their cell, his low voice familiar. Unlike the guards, this man's eyes weren't blank. But they were pitiless.

"Rezi Soresh," Leia said coolly.

He bowed his head in acknowledgment.

Leia glowered at him. "Where's Luke?"

Han couldn't believe she was holding so steady. Leia could be a real pain sometimes, but he had to admit, she was good in a crisis. He'd never met anyone as tough as she was — or as frustrating. But in this case, stubbornness was the one thing that might keep them alive.

"Don't worry about Luke," Soresh said. "He'll be taken care of. As will you — and your precious Rebel fleet."

Leia jumped to her feet, fists balled. Han knew she refused to let *anyone* threaten the fleet — even if there was nothing she could do about it. "What's that supposed to mean?"

"It means you're luckier than you know," Soresh said. His lips parted in a gruesome smile. "You won't have to see the destruction of everything and everyone you care about."

"Yeah, and why's that?" Han asked. He had a bad feeling he already knew the answer.

Soresh's smile widened, confirming his suspicions. "Because by the time it happens, you'll all be dead."

Luke screamed.

The interrogator droid hovered before him, manipulator arms hard at work.

He had felt pain before. But that was nothing compared to this. There was no word for this.

Only screams.

There was no sleep.

Sometimes he passed out — from the pain, from the hunger, from exhaustion. But always, he was jolted back into consciousness. Blinding lights flashed at all hours; deafening noise made his head pound night and day. He had never been so tired. Too tired to think. Almost too tired to feel.

We have to break you down before we can build you up, Soresh said.

The commander visited the cell sometimes. Luke didn't know how often. There was no way of keeping time in the cell, no way of knowing how many hours and days had passed. It was beginning to seem as if he'd been a prisoner forever. But whenever Soresh did come, he brought gifts. Sometimes food. Sometimes a serum that would allow a few precious hours of unconsciousness. Sometimes, at his command, just a temporary end to the torture. But it always began again, as soon as Soresh walked away.

Luke knew the Imperial was responsible for all of this. And so Luke hated him.

But he was beginning to look forward to Soresh's visits. He was too tired to escape or think about revenge. All he hoped for anymore was a few minutes of peace.

And soon, each day, all day, he hoped for Soresh.

Luke huddled against the wall of the cell, shivering. The temperature had been lowered to only a few degrees above freezing. His breath misted in the frosty air.

"Hello, Luke," Soresh said, his face appearing like magic beyond the bars. "Having a good day?"

Luke didn't answer. He had learned to conserve his strength.

"I brought you something to eat," Soresh said. He slipped a muja fruit through the bars.

Luke pounced on it like a starved profrogg.

"You're doing very well," Soresh said. "It might soon be time for Phase Two. Would you like that?"

Again, Luke didn't answer. He gnawed on the fruit. It was soft and overripe, with a sour undertaste. Even so, it was still the best muja fruit he'd ever eaten.

"I take no joy in your pain," Soresh said. "I'd be happy to let you out of here at any time. All you have to do is swear your allegiance to me. Then all the pain will end."

Luke wanted to make that happen.

Remember Uncle Owen and Aunt Beru, he thought weakly. *Remember Ben.*

They had given their lives for him. So he could *fight* the Empire, not join it.

But he had no fight left in him.

"You're all alone here, Luke," Soresh said. "Your friends have abandoned you. There's no one left to save you . . . except for me. Join me and save yourself."

Your friends.

Luke drew in a deep, painful breath. *Remember Han,* he told himself.

Remember Leia.

"Never," he whispered. His voice was hoarse from screaming. He repeated it, louder, more sure. "Never."

Soresh shrugged. "So be it." He turned his back on the cell and began walking away.

Luke panicked — what if he never came back? What if this was the end of the little visits and treats that kept him alive? What if Soresh just left him to die?

But Soresh stopped, and turned back. "Oh, if you're worried about what your friends will think of you if you give in to me, don't. They're long gone."

"They would never leave me," Luke croaked.

"Perhaps you're right," Soresh agreed. "They say the dead stay with us forever." He peered around the empty cell as if hunting for ghosts. "Who knows, maybe they're here with us right now."

No. Luke refused to believe it. "You're lying."

"I had no use for them," Soresh said coldly. "*You're* the special one. *You're* the one I want. They were just nuisances. And so I disposed of them. Don't worry — someday, you'll thank me."

Soresh strode through the underground tunnels, eager to return to his office. While some equipment and personnel were housed on the surface of the moon, the bulk of his operation lay in the tunnels. He had discovered them in his early explorations of the moon, grateful to the civilization that carved them millennia before.

Luke's treatment was progressing even faster than Soresh had hoped. He was convinced that telling Luke his friends were dead would push the Rebel over the edge. Soresh had honed this process over two decades. He knew exactly how to tear apart a man's brain and rebuild it to his liking. First you broke them down. Fear, sleeplessness, pain, starvation — they were all crucial ingredients, doled out in precise amounts. You stripped away everything the prisoner had, made them understand that they were completely alone, with no one left to save them.

No one but their master, Rezi Soresh.

Once they understood this, they were ready for the next phase.

Years ago, the process had been more complicated. Soresh had created men like X-7, who were completely obedient to Soresh but could still think for themselves. Clearly, that was a mistake. Even a little bit of independence could lead to disaster. So now Soresh had refined the process. Not that he'd had much choice — time was short, resources were few. So he'd found some shortcuts. The soldiers he'd created didn't have X-7's strategic capabilities, and they wouldn't be much use on independent missions. But when it came to carrying out simple tasks and doing exactly what Soresh ordered them to do, they were perfect.

Of course there had been a few missteps along the way. A few mistakes he'd had to dispose of. But now he knew exactly what he was doing. The men guarding the base were completely under his control. The Rebel spy he'd brainwashed had passed along the fake Imperial transmission to his Rebel leaders, just as Soresh commanded. And now Luke was well on his way to becoming the most powerful servant Soresh could ever have.

With a Jedi under his control, no one would be able to stop him. Not even Darth Vader.

And when he destroyed the Rebel fleet — and Darth Vader along with it — the Emperor would have no choice but to forgive him. He would take his rightful place at the Emperor's side.

It was time to put the plan into action. He activated the comm system, and opened a channel to Darth Vader's private line. Only a few people in the galaxy knew how to reach the Dark Lord directly. But Soresh had always known more than people suspected.

Darth Vader's inky black hood appeared on the screen. His heavy, rhythmic breathing seemed so close, Soresh could almost imagine the puff of hot air against his ear. He nearly shuddered, but forced himself to remain steady. Vader couldn't hurt him now.

"You cannot evade me for long," Vader said. The deep, rumbling vibration of his voice rippled through Soresh. He remembered the rumors he had heard, that Vader could suck the life out of someone with a mere thought, even through a viewscreen. Even from halfway across the galaxy.

Silly stories, Soresh reminded himself. *Show no fear.*

"I don't plan to for much longer," he said. "After all, I have something you want. And if you follow my instructions to the letter, I might let you have it."

"All I want is your corpse," Vader said. "And soon, I shall have it."

The transmission cut out.

Soresh smiled. Perfect. The comm operated on an encrypted channel, but Vader would easily trace its source to the Sixela system. Which meant that he would be right in the neighborhood when Soresh was finally ready for him.

Fear and rumor were powerful weapons, and Vader used them well. But they were nothing against *real* weapons, and Soresh had one of the most powerful ones in the galaxy under his control. He suspected that even Vader didn't know about Maw Installation, the secret research base devoted to creating superweapons. Grand Moff Tarkin had established and supervised it. Its secrets had died with him. But Soresh knew, because Soresh had made it his business to know everything. Including the existence and location of Maw Installation — and which of its scientists could be easily blackmailed.

As an Imperial Commander he had been in charge of following the flow of credits, making sure all contracts were paid in full, all docs were in order. It was a job few respected. A job for a weak man, they'd thought. They didn't understand that Soresh's job was *information*. And the only thing more powerful than information was the weapon being built at Maw Installation.

The weapon whose prototype was just on the other side of the wall. Soresh couldn't unleash the weapon on the Rebel base itself — not until he was sure it would work. But it had been so simple to lure the Rebel fleet to *him.* Now the weapon sat in its launch bay, waiting for its moment. It was an instrument of total destruction.

Just like me, Soresh thought. *Come find me, Vader. Come and meet your destiny.*

And your doom.

It was not possible. Not possible that Han was dead. That Chewbacca was dead. Leia was dead. That Luke would never see any of them again.

It was not possible.

But he believed it was true.

Soresh had taught him that anything was possible here. Anything except escape — anything except hope.

I'm a Jedi, Luke told himself. *I have the power of the Force.*

But what good was that? Even if he knew how to use his powers, he didn't know what he would do with them. Ben had shown him how to levitate small objects, how to deflect laserblasts with his eyes closed. But surely even Ben didn't have the power to escape from a place like this. Even Ben couldn't save his friends, if his friends were already dead.

Ben would tell me to be strong, Luke thought.

"Stay strong," he whispered, as if hearing the words out loud would make them easier to follow. But his voice was weak, and it only reminded him that he, too, was weak. If only Obi-Wan were here to tell him. To *guide* him, to show him how to save himself. If only he could imagine Ben's voice assuring him that he would survive this, then maybe he would believe it.

Luke closed his eyes, trying to summon the memory of his old friend. Ben had spoken to him before in times of crisis, assuring him of his strength. Reminding him of his destiny.

But it was no use.

His mind was too clouded by grief, by fear, by exhaustion. There was too much noise in the cell and in his head. Ben was gone, like Han and Leia were gone, like everyone was gone. The only voice that could help him was his own.

"You need me."

Ferus smiled at the familiar voice. "How did you know?" He had been lying in his bunk, eyes closed, trying to sort through his dilemma. Now he sat up to face the flickering, translucent spirit of a fallen Jedi.

"When your heart and mind are open to the Force, they are open to me," Obi-Wan said.

Ferus still didn't understand how the Jedi Master was able to speak to him from beyond the grave. But he was grateful. Knowing Obi-Wan was out there, watching, made every challenge easier to bear.

"Luke is in trouble," Obi-Wan said. "And I fear for his sister, too."

Ferus stifled his irritation with the old man. Obi-Wan would never have admitted it, but for him, Leia always came second. An afterthought.

"I know," Ferus said. "They've been missing for nearly a week. I've begun to fear the worst."

"You can help them," Obi-Wan said. "You know the way."

"I know the way?" Ferus repeated. This wasn't exactly the help he'd been hoping for. "You're the mysterious spirit who knows all — don't *you* know the way? Tell me how to help them. Tell me *where* to find them!"

Obi-Wan shook his head, "There is a disturbance in the Force surrounding Luke. His connection to it is growing weaker. I cannot help him. Only you can."

"I have no idea where they are," Ferus said. "If I knew, don't you think I'd be halfway there by now?"

"But you have your suspicions," Obi-Wan said. It wasn't a question.

Ferus hesitated. He had drawn the connections in his mind, but hadn't yet said them out loud. It was as General Dodonna said — he had no evidence, only his instincts. And his instincts had been wrong before, with dire consequences. "I fear the Rebels are walking into a trap," he said slowly. "And that Luke and Leia's disappearance has something to do with it. This deserted moon where the Rebels hope to ambush the Imperials . . ."

"You believe that to be where you'll find Luke and Leia," Obi-Wan finished for him.

Ferus nodded.

"And yet you sit here, doing nothing."

Obi-Wan had always known how to make him feel better — and how to make him feel the opposite.

"The things I've done in the past . . ." Ferus broke off. It pained him too much to think about the choices he'd made — choices that had led to the death of his best friend, Roan Lands. To the death of so many others. He had trusted his instincts; he had trusted the wrong people. They had paid the price for his mistakes.

"Sometimes not choosing is itself a choice," Obi-Wan added. "By not acting, you act."

"Tell me what to do," Ferus pleaded. He felt like a Padawan again, scrambling for crumbs at his Master's feet. And part of him wished for those old days, when the way ahead had seemed so certain. When every question had an answer.

Obi-Wan favored him with a familiar wry smile. "You know I can't do that. I can only tell you to believe —"

"— in the Force," Ferus cut in, irritated. "I know."

Obi-Wan's smile widened. "Actually, I was going to suggest you believe in yourself. But then, I suppose in the end, it's all the same thing."

CHAPTER EIGHT

Luke sat perfectly still as Soresh strapped him into the chair. The durasteel was cold against his skin. Sharp-edged restraints wrapped around his ankles, his wrists, his waist, his neck, and his forehead, holding him in place. Slowly and carefully, Soresh attached a series of sensors to Luke's forehead. "Nothing to fear," he said. "This won't hurt at all."

Luke was far past fearing pain.

Soresh raised an injector. "This is just something to ease the process along and make everything go more smoothly. You want that, don't you?"

Luke stared blankly ahead. Soresh smiled as if he had responded. "Good." He injected the serum into Luke's neck.

There was a faint pinprick of pain, and then nothing. A numbness spread through his body.

"The serum and the machinery work together," Soresh said, sounding proud. "I designed them myself. They act on the memory centers of your brain. Think of it as a million thermo missiles launched into your bloodstream. Except instead of heat, they're seeking memories. Seek and destroy, that's their mission. Every painful moment of your past, every person who's ever betrayed you, ever abandoned you, all gone. Everything that's made you who you are. One by one, we're going to purge you of such unpleasant attachments. We're going to wash the slate clean and leave you pure and fresh. As empty and trouble-free as the day you were born. Won't that be nice?"

Luke was having trouble keeping track of the words. They skidded past him, just out of reach, turning to nonsense syllables. He knew Soresh was saying something important, something that should terrify him. But the voice seemed so distant. Everything seemed distant. Luke felt like he was floating away.

He was on Tatooine, drawing spaceships in the sand, dreaming of the stars.

He was waking up on a barren cliffside, looking into the face of a crazy hermit he barely knew. Learning the secret truth of his past. "I was once a Jedi Knight," the old man said. "The same as your father."

• • •

He was surrounded by strange sights and sounds in a Mos Eisley cantina, trying not to get himself killed. Trying to buy passage to the Alderaan system from a smooth-talking spacer who called himself Han Solo.

He was on the bridge of the *Millennium Falcon*, searching for a planet that was no longer there.

He was bursting into an Imperial prison cell. A woman — a princess — lay asleep on a bare metal slab. She wore a long, white gown and was the most beautiful thing he'd ever seen.

He was watching a red lightsaber slice through Ben's empty cloak.

He was at the controls of his X-wing, stars twinkling in his viewscreen, the Death Star looming. He was one with the ship, one with the Force. He was squeezing his fingers around the trigger, knowing with absolute certainty that his aim was true.

He was in the dark.

"Hold on, Luke. Please."

It was Leia's voice. But not Leia's face. There were no

faces in the black depths of his mind, the only place he could hide from Soresh's memory missiles. The darkness left behind as, one by one, everything and everyone was stripped away.

There won't be anything left of me, Luke thought, clinging to his memories, to himself. It was like grasping a cloud—nothing to hold on to but empty air.

"Use the Force, Luke," Ben's voice said, echoing in the emptiness.

Use it for what? Luke cried from the depths of his mind.

"Trust the Force. Trust your feelings. Trust yourself."

And then the voices of his friends faded away, drowned out by a new voice. Soresh's voice, deep and commanding. "You are nothing," it said. "You belong to me. Your Master."

The voice filled the darkness, until it consumed everything; it was Luke's entire world.

"You are nothing," it repeated, again and again.

"You belong to me."

It would be so easy to stop fighting, to let go of the memories and the pain. To believe the voice—to let it replace his own.

Hold on, Luke told himself desperately. *For Leia. For Ben.*

For me.

• • •

The treatment was hard on mind and body. Some took days to recover. Some never did.

Luke lay unconscious for several hours, and Soresh stayed by his side, waiting. He had waited months for this moment. But now every additional minute was torture. He was so close to his goal, he could taste it. And, finally, the Rebel stirred. His eyes flickered open, and he bolted upright on the cot, alarmed.

The guards at the door raised their blasters, but Soresh stilled them with a look. He placed a hand on Luke's shoulder. "Easy," he said. "Lie down. You're safe. Your body's had quite a shock. Take your time."

Luke obeyed without question.

It was a good sign.

Soresh watched the monitors carefully, tracking Luke's heart rate, his breathing, his brain waves. Soon they'd all stabilized within normal parameters. It was time to begin. "Sit up," Soresh said.

Luke sat up.

"Who are you?" Soresh asked.

Luke opened his mouth — then hesitated. He looked confused. "I don't know."

"What is your purpose?" Soresh asked.

When the answer came, it was slow and halting, but it was correct. "To serve you."

"And who am I?"

"My Master." Luke's voice was blank, his eyes dull.

"Where do you come from?" Soresh asked.

"I don't know," Luke said. "Do you know?"

"You come from nowhere," Soresh prompted him. "You are no one."

Luke nodded. "I come from nowhere. I am no one."

"What do you remember of your past? Think hard."

Luke shook his head. "Nothing."

"Very good." Soresh patted him on the shoulder again. This had gone even better than he'd expected. Perhaps there was something about the Jedi that made their minds particularly weak. Or perhaps this one was just eager to give up. "Lie down again, relax, sleep. Soon you'll be ready for another treatment, and we'll begin again."

uke's lightsaber sliced the air, a blur of motion. He whirled and spun, slashing at anything that moved. Training droids bobbed awkwardly through the training room, trying to dodge the glowing blade. But it was useless. Luke was everywhere at once. Severed mechanical limbs, joint couplings, servomotors, and broken antennas flew across the room, dislodged by the whirling lightsaber. It was as if the blade was the living thing, and Luke its servant. The blade danced with deadly grace, and one droid after another clattered to the floor. Still, Luke pushed on, hacking, slicing, killing.

Exactly as he'd been ordered to do.

"Enough!" Soresh shouted.

Abruptly, Luke froze. His arm dropped to his side, deactivating the lightsaber.

"Return your weapon to me," Soresh ordered.

Luke surrendered it without hesitation.

Soresh surveyed the broken droids strewn across the training room, and the Jedi standing in the middle, seemingly unaware of the destruction he'd wrought.

My Jedi, Soresh thought, pleased. He had been slightly worried that his control over Luke would interfere with the Jedi's ability to use the Force. But so far, there had been no such problems. After several days of testing, Luke hadn't failed to complete a single challenge. Soresh had never had a new subject this obedient — or this powerful. A ring of armed guards surrounded him at all times, ready to step in if the prisoner got out of control. But Luke never got out of control. *Control* was the only thing his empty mind had left.

"I believe you're ready for your final test," Soresh told Luke. "Would you like that?" It often entertained him to treat the subjects as if they could still form opinions of their own.

"Does it please you?" Luke asked. There was no curiosity in his voice, or any emotion at all.

"It does." It was true. Once he ensured Luke's absolute obedience and loyalty, he could move forward with the final phase of his plan.

"Then it pleases me," Luke said flatly.

"Good." Soresh turned to his guards. "We'll meet you on the surface," he ordered them. "Bring the prisoners."

• • •

"This can't be good," Leia muttered, as the guards shackled the prisoners together with heavy chains and marched them out of the cell.

"Cheer up, Princess," Han said. "Maybe they've seen the errors of their ways and they're taking us back to our ship."

But she didn't smile at the weak joke, and neither did he. Durasteel shackles seemed an odd way of saying, "Sorry for locking you in a dungeon for two weeks."

"Where do you think they're taking us, Han?" Leia asked.

He detected only the faintest quiver of fear in her voice. But it was enough to make him lie. "No idea, Princess. Your guess is as good as mine."

In fact, he had a pretty good guess. His gut was telling him that once they left this cell, they wouldn't be coming back. In fact, he was beginning to think they wouldn't be going much of anywhere, unless it was in a box. He reached forward and squeezed Leia's hand, just once.

The surface was even more arid and empty than Han remembered. But it felt good to feel the wind on his face again — even if it would be for the last time.

Chewbacca let out a mournful roar.

"Silence!" the guard shouted.

"I know, buddy," Han said softly. "Me, too."

Two figures stood a few meters from the doorway, waiting. Leia gasped. "Luke!" she cried.

He was standing beside Soresh, arms hanging loosely at his sides. As far as Han could tell, he wasn't in chains or cuffs or any kind of restraints. And yet he just stood there, staring blankly ahead.

"Luke!" Leia screamed, as the guards marched them right past Luke and Soresh.

"Who are they?" Han heard Luke ask.

"Miscreants," Soresh said. "And it's their time to die."

He handed Luke a blaster. The guards shoved Han, Leia, and Chewbacca against the side of a small shed.

I can take them, Han thought. If he could just distract them for a second —

"Don't," Leia murmured, catching his eye. "Not yet. Luke has a plan. He must."

"Luke? You mean the guy standing by Soresh, holding the blaster? The one acting like he's never seen us before?"

"Luke would never hurt us," Leia said with determination. "You know that."

Luke raised the blaster and took aim.

"I know that, Princess, but . . ." But how could Han tell her about the look he'd seen in Luke's eyes, the look that reminded him so much of X-7? She was right, *Luke* would never hurt them. But Han wasn't so sure Luke was in there anymore.

Chewbacca growled, and glanced meaningfully at the nearest guard's blaster. He was holding it loosely, keeping his eyes on Soresh — and paying a dangerously small amount of attention to the angry Wookiee standing a couple meters away.

"On three," Han murmured under his breath, steeling himself to make a move. "One . . . two . . ."

"Now!" Soresh shouted.

Luke fired.

CHAPTER TEN

The shot went wild, slamming into the wall half a meter above Han's ear. At the same moment, a deafening burst of music exploded behind them. Traditional Aridinian folk music — famous across the galaxy for its ability to make human ears bleed after just a few notes. The guards' attention flickered toward the source of the torturous noise. It was exactly the opportunity Han and Chewbacca needed, and they leapt into action. Chewbacca knocked his guard over with a single sweep of his massive paw, seizing the man's blaster in the same motion. Han and his guard collapsed to the ground, rolling through the dirt, their fists flying.

A lumbering speeder truck rolled out from behind a nearby building, heading straight toward them. A golden protocol droid was at the controls, while behind him, a small silver-and-blue astromech blasted folk music from his internal speakers. And neither the speeder nor the music showed any sign of braking. Guards and prisoners alike scattered out of its way.

"Nice job, for tin cans," Han muttered, launching himself at the two guards holding Leia in place. He wrapped an arm around each of their necks, choking the life out of them. Leia darted in to grab their weapons, tossing one to Han. He dropped the guards and snatched the blaster, ready for a fight.

Soresh had scuttled away somewhere like a Rylothean schutta. Luke was nowhere to be seen. But there was little time to search for either: The area was crawling with guards and the air was already thick with smoke. Laserfire streaked across the camp. The speeder truck wheeled in circles. C-3PO had found himself a blaster, and was peppering laserbolts in every direction with little chance of hitting anything. Han ran for cover, blasting enemies in his wake. "Behind you, Chewie!" he shouted, as the Wookiee whirled around and took out three guards with one blow of his massive forearms. Han ducked behind a low shed, peeking around the edge to fire an occasional shot. He spotted Chewbacca and Leia slipping into a similar hiding place about fifty meters away.

Han checked his remaining ammunition, then prepared to make a run for it. Beyond the small complex there was nothing but wide-open space, dotted with gigantic boulders, rocky outcrops, and no sign of civilization. They had less than a kilometer of ground to cover, and they'd be safe. Or at least, safer.

"Here goes nothing," Han muttered — and then froze.

The telltale pressure of a blaster muzzle jutted into the back of his head. "Don't move," a flat voice behind him said. Then: "On your knees!"

"Make up your mind," Han grumbled. But he lowered himself to his knees. And then steeled himself for what came next. "Takes a real man to shoot someone in the back," he muttered.

But as he'd expected, the guard didn't react. Apparently brainwashing didn't improve small talk skills.

"Well, what are you waiting for?" he snapped. If this was going to be the end, there was no point in stalling. He readied himself to strike, even if there was little chance of success. There was no way he was ending up back in one of those cells, waiting for an execution. He'd fight till his last breath before he ended up down there again.

Before Han could act, there was an explosive burst of laserfire . . . but no pain.

And he was still kneeling. The blaster at his head fell away. Han turned around to find a guard lying in the dirt, dead. Luke was standing over him, blaster in hand. A thin trail of smoke drifted up from its muzzle.

"You okay?" Luke asked, grasping Han's hand and pulling him to his feet.

"Luke?" Han said, unsure whether to be alarmed or relieved. "You know who I am?"

"Of course I know who you are," Luke said, dragging Han farther out of sight behind the buildings. Leia and Chewbacca were firing constantly as they backed toward safety. The guards all cowered behind buildings and boulders of their own, firing sporadically.

Han was very relieved to see Luke acting like Luke again. Almost as relieved as he was not to be dead. "So before . . . ?"

"An act," Luke confirmed. "I have to let Soresh think he's won. It's the only way to find out what he's up to."

"I think we found out," Han said. "He's up to killing us. So how about we make a break before he tries again." The *Falcon* was docked nearby, and Han was certain they could take out the guards and get them-selves off this rock. *All* of them.

But Luke shook his head.

"It's not just us," Luke said. "Some of the things I've heard — Soresh is plotting something against the Rebel fleet. I'm sure of it."

Han had suspected the same thing. "All the more reason to get out of here, kid. Fly away, save the day, be home for dinner."

"I have to stay," Luke said, with quiet intensity. "I just . . . I feel like this is where I need to be. That staying could be the only way to save them."

"This more of your Jedi mumbo jumbo?" Han grumbled.

"This is my gut," Luke said.

And Han couldn't argue with that. He pressed a comlink into Luke's hands. "You call us when you need us," he said gruffly, trying not to reveal how worried he was. The kid was taking a big burden upon himself, and Han wasn't sure he could handle it. He wasn't sure anyone could. "We'll be waiting."

"Thanks," Luke said. "Now, I need one more thing."

"Anything, kid."

Luke hesitated. "You trust me?"

Han didn't like the sound of that. "About as much as I trust anyone," he allowed. Which wasn't saying much. "What do you need?"

Luke gave him a thin smile. "I need you to shoot me."

Luke lay on the ground, a gaping blaster wound in his left shoulder. He barely felt the pain. Instead, there was only joy and relief in the knowledge that his friends were alive. And not just alive—free. Knowing that made what he had to do so much easier to bear. Now that he knew they were safe, he could play Soresh's game, he could pretend to be a blank and obedient slave for as long as it took. There was hope after all—for his friends, for the Rebel fleet, and for himself.

He heard footsteps approach, and closed his eyes. Moments later, a booted toe dug into his side. "Huh?" he said weakly, pretending to be waking from unconsciousness. Soresh stood over him, eyes fiery with rage. Two guards stood behind him.

"He escaped," Luke admitted, then moaned.

"Not before giving you a little parting gift, I see," Soresh said, gesturing to the wound. "Nice friends you have there."

"Friends?" Luke asked, careful to sound confused, but not curious.

"Never mind." Soresh cleared his throat. "I'll admit this didn't work out as I'd hoped, but at least you've proved your loyalty. I'm proud of you."

"Thank you," Luke said.

"Of course, you failed to accomplish your mission," Soresh said sternly. "And for that, you must be punished."

Luke forced himself not to react. *Leia and Han are safe*, he thought. *That's what matters.*

Soresh jerked his head at the guards, who grabbed Luke and hoisted him roughly off the ground. "Take him inside and teach him not to fail me again."

CHAPTER ELEVEN

The Firespray craft slipped out of hyperdrive at the edge of the Sixela star system. Div steered the ship toward the sixth planet from the sun, which was circled by a small red moon. It felt good to be flying again — he'd been stuck on the ground for far too long. And when it came to flying, there was nothing like piloting a Firespray. Not that there was anything wrong with the Alliance's X-wings. But the Firespray had long been Div's favorite ship. Sleek, swift, and modified for optimal speed and firing capacities, it was a ship well suited to the galaxy's best pilots. And Div had always considered himself the best of the best.

From the copilot seat, Ferus activated the long-range sensors, and tried to secure a visual on their target.

"Doesn't look like much," Div said, as they reached the moon.

"Let's hope it's not," Ferus replied.

Div knew he was right. If their suspicions proved wrong, if there was nothing here but dim sun and bare rock, it would be for the best. But he couldn't help secretly wishing for a little action. Until recently, Div had been a mercenary pilot, the best in the galaxy. He'd hired himself out to anyone who'd come calling, hopping from one dirty job to the next. Smuggling, airlifting, sneak attacks, he'd done it all — and he'd done it well. Life had been a nonstop stream of fiery battles and breathless escapes. Just the way Div liked it. Because the faster he moved, the less he had to think.

Running into Ferus again had been like running into a duracrete wall. It stopped him cold. For months, he'd been stuck on that humid Rebel moon, digging ditches and chopping trees and doing *nothing*. Nothing except thinking about his past, and everything he'd lost. Sometimes he wished he could just erase it all — Clive, Astri, Trever, all the dead, all the losses, all the painful memories — just start fresh. Since that was impossible, he did the next best thing. He flew fast, he hit hard, he defied death in a thousand different ways, anything to distract himself. And there were no distractions on Yavin 4. There was only Ferus, that constant reminder of the past.

So the rational part of him hoped they didn't run into any trouble on this moon.

But the other part of him — the part that was desperate for distraction, for movement, for *action* — almost hoped they did.

"Bringing us into orbit," Div said, dropping the ship so low it nearly skimmed the atmosphere.

"Laser cannons armed," Ferus reported. "Just in case."

Div tried to reach out with the Force and sense whether there was danger lurking beneath them. But he felt nothing — as usual. Ferus kept assuring him that with time and practice, he might regain the abilities he'd had as a child. *The Force is always with you*, Ferus kept saying. *You just have to let it in.* But as hard as Div tried, he felt nothing. He could remember how effortless it had been when he was young, when all he had to do was open his mind and he could do *anything*. He just couldn't remember how he had done it. And the harder he tried, the more impossible it seemed.

"Do you sense anything?" he finally asked, giving up.

Ferus inclined his head, as if listening to the silence of space. Then he shook his head. "There is something, some small disturbance in the Force . . . but I don't believe we're in danger. Yet."

The Rebel Command would be furious if they knew Div and Ferus had ventured here, ahead of the mission. Reconnaissance had been deemed too dangerous, for fear of tipping off the Imperials who might already be here.

General Dodonna didn't want anything interfering with the mission. But there were no other ships in sight, and no sign of an Imperial presence on the radar.

"Then I'm bringing her down a little lower," Div said. He dropped the ship into the thin atmosphere. Wispy clouds whipped past the viewscreen.

"There!" Ferus cried, pointing down at the surface.

"What?" Div asked.

"Something," Ferus said, shaking his head. "There's something there, I feel it."

At this speed, it was little more than a blur. Div saw nothing of use or interest. But Jedi saw things that others did not. And so Div slowed the ship for the next pass around the planet, aiming the sensor array at the general area Ferus had picked out. And there it was: the *Millennium Falcon*.

Div's eyes widened. He was about to take the Firespray in for a landing, when Ferus stayed his hand. "Not yet," he said. "Look." The ship was circled by a ring of men, standing in a tight formation. There was no indication Han, Leia, or Chewbacca were among them. "We have to know more."

So they circled the moon several more times. The instruments detected signs of life, all of them concentrated in a ten-kilometer radius of squat duracrete buildings.

Ferus drummed his fingers on the control panel. "Perhaps it's time to find out —"

A low beeping from the comm cut him off.

"It's a distress signal," Ferus reported. "And it's being transmitted on a Rebel frequency."

"It must be the *Falcon*," Div said, certain there were no other Rebels in the system. But the signal originated several kilometers away from where the Corellian freighter was docked. Div took the ship in for a landing. Then he armed his blaster. Maybe the distress call was coming from the *Falcon* crew. But there was always a chance someone else had gotten their hands on the Rebel frequencies. And Div had no intention of walking into a trap. "Ready?" he asked.

Ferus nodded. He activated his lightsaber, and opened the hatchway. They climbed down to the surface of the moon. It was an arid, craggy landscape of shallow craters and towering boulders. As they explored the area, their footsteps kicked up clouds of fine red dust. The distress signal was coming from this location, there was no doubt about it. Whatever had called them here was nearby — right on top of them.

"We mean you no harm!" Div shouted, trying to draw them out. "Unless you mean some to us," he added, under his breath. He fingered his blaster trigger, ready for anything.

"We've found them," Ferus said quietly.

Div didn't bother to ask how he could be so sure. And he wasn't surprised when, a moment later, Han,

Leia, and the Wookiee appeared from behind a boulder. The golden protocol droid and his counterpart were by their side.

Han flashed a crooked smile. "Took you long enough."

"What do you mean, Luke decided to *stay*?" Ferus asked, sounding alarmed.

The six of them — plus one very uncomfortable Wookiee — were crammed inside the Firespray. Han and Leia had run through the highlights of their time on the moon. Div couldn't believe the situation was even *worse* than he'd feared.

"He thought it was the only way to figure out Soresh's plans," Leia explained. "So he's pretending to be under Soresh's control."

"A double agent," Ferus said, under his breath. All the color had drained out of his face. "He has to escape — before it's too late."

"Hey, I tried to convince him," Han said. "The kid knows what he wants. I say we trust him."

"If Luke believes he can do it . . ." Leia began.

Ferus shook his head. "Believing in one's own strength can be a great asset. But it can also be the key to defeat."

"It's really too bad you never got to meet Luke's crazy Jedi friend," Han said. "You two could have talked riddles to each other all day long."

Ferus didn't seem to hear him. Div watched his old

friend closely, suspecting he was lost in the past. There was a time when Ferus himself had acted as a double agent, confident that he was strong enough to face the challenge. He had drawn sharp boundaries between the man he was and the man he was pretending to be. But as time passed, the boundaries blurred. The dark side swelled within him. He had looked the same, acted the same — but those who knew him well had sensed a difference. A hard, angry edge that had never been there before. A darkness. Ferus had come close to giving in to the dark side. Closer than anyone knew, Ferus had once admitted to Div. It was Div that had saved him — Div, and everything he had once represented. Hope for the future: innocence and light. That was a long time ago, another life, when Div was known as Lune, when Ferus was a leader. It was a long-dead past, but maybe Div wasn't the only one who still bore the scars.

"Luke has great power," Ferus said. "If he succumbs, and the Empire gains control over him . . ."

"He won't," Leia said firmly. "They won't."

"How can you be sure?" Ferus asked.

"Because I know Luke." Leia glared at him for a long moment. It seemed like Ferus was wrestling with a response. But ultimately, he stayed silent, and looked away.

Div cleared his throat, hoping to cut through the tension. "We have to warn the fleet," he pointed out. "They're flying into a trap."

"What do you think we've been trying to do?" Han said. But their weak distress signal had barely made it out of the atmosphere. And accessing the *Millennium Falcon*'s communications system was out of the question. Once the prisoners had escaped, Soresh had tripled the guard on the ship.

Now they had the Firespray. Leia fired up the comm system and contacted Yavin 4. The news wasn't good: The fleet was already on its way. There was no way of warning them while they were traveling at lightspeed.

"This is my fault," Ferus murmured. "I delayed too long. Again."

Div wanted to reassure him, but didn't have the words. And really, Ferus was right. They had both delayed too long — and now the entire fleet could suffer the consequences. "So we do what we can from here," Div said. "I figure we're nearly a day ahead of the fleet. That gives us time to find out exactly what kind of trap Soresh is setting —"

"— and shut it down," Han said, his fingers already itching for his blaster. Div suspected the spacer was as eager for action as he was. The two of them understood each other — in another life, they might even have been friends. But Div had long ago vowed to have no more friends. You couldn't lose what you didn't have. Now he only had comrades in arms, and he was glad to count Han among them.

I am nothing.
I am no one.
I belong to you.

The mantra ran through Luke's mind on a constant loop. It was the only way to keep his eyes blank, his voice flat, his face clear of anything that might give away the truth. Even now, Soresh watched him carefully for any flicker of independence or disloyalty. But Luke had gotten good at walking through the motions of slavery. He didn't know how he'd found the strength to resist Soresh's brainwashing, just as he didn't know where he'd found the strength to keep up the act for this long. But somehow, he had. Somewhere, deep in him, there was something that refused to bend. A voice that told him to hold on, no matter what. It was no voice he'd ever heard before — more than anything, it sounded like his own. Only deeper. Stronger. Sometimes Luke wondered if it was his father, helping him from beyond the grave.

"Welcome to my greatest masterpiece," Soresh said, ushering Luke into a large room lined with computers. A giant viewscreen covered one entire wall. "Today I reclaim my rightful place at the Emperor's side. All thanks to you."

Soresh loved nothing more than boasting about his plans to the obedient guards who followed him everywhere. Ever since Luke's final "proof" of loyalty, he had been Soresh's favored audience. And yet Luke still had no idea what he was planning for the Rebel fleet — or how to stop it.

The Commander activated the comm unit. Moments later, Darth Vader himself appeared on the screen. The image was larger than life, nearly three meters high. Luke suppressed a shudder. Even through a screen, the Dark Lord was a terrifying sight. And it wasn't just terror Luke needed to suppress. It was rage. Every time Luke saw that dark mask, every time he heard that deadly even breathing, he saw the red blade of a lightsaber lashing down on Ben. And the rage overwhelmed him.

Hold on, urged the voice that might have belonged to his father. *You can do this.*

He could. He stood motionless and empty before the Dark Lord, letting Soresh play out his mad game. And as soon as Soresh's attention was fixed on the viewscreen, he slipped his hand into his sleeve, where he'd hidden Han's comlink. He activated it, opening a channel to his friends. Now anything he heard, they would hear, too.

"I told you I had something you wanted," Soresh said, smiling up at the screen. "Here he is."

Darth Vader said nothing. But his fury radiated in waves. Luke could almost feel the room growing warmer.

"Tell the Dark Lord how much you're looking forward to meeting him," Soresh commanded Luke.

"If it pleases my Master, I look forward to meeting you," Luke said obediently. He was surprised — playing along with Soresh wasn't hard at all. With every command, it became easier to comply.

"You will soon regret your impudence," Darth Vader said. The screen went dark.

Soresh burst into laughter.

It was all Luke could do not to gape at him. Vader's rage had been known to drive men to panic, to madness, even to death, but never to . . . joy?

"You see?" Soresh cackled. "Everything according to plan. He's tracing our coordinates as we speak. If I've calculated correctly — and I *always* calculate correctly — he'll arrive just in time to greet your Rebel fleet. I'm almost tempted to delay a bit, just for the joy of watching Vader blown up by a sky full of Rebel scum." He shook his head, briskly. "But that would be indulgent. No, I can't let personal feelings interfere with carefully set timing. Vader will burn along with the rest of them, that will have to be enough for me."

"Vader will burn," Luke repeated, hoping to help the monologue along. He needed more details — *something* that would help him figure out what to do when it was finally time to act.

"That tends to be what happens when the sun goes supernova," Soresh said, nearly giggling.

He really was insane, Luke realized, if he thought he had control over the sun. Silexa was a blue giant star. It would go supernova someday, most likely — but not for several million years.

Luke waited for Soresh to continue, but the explanation never came. Instead, Soresh settled into a chair and kicked his feet up on one of the large, gray instrument panels. "Now, we wait."

They waited so long Luke began swaying on his legs, exhausted from standing for so long. But the guards still stood rigidly at attention, oblivious to their own exhaustion. Luke did his best to match them.

I could attack him at any time, he thought — although with all the guards standing around, he and Soresh would likely die together. Luke wasn't afraid to die. But he was afraid to die for nothing. And that's what it would be, if he attacked before he knew exactly what Soresh had planned.

"There!" Soresh shouted, leaping to his feet.

The viewscreen was filled with stars — but as Luke watched, one of the stars grew brighter and divided into two, then five, then a hundred.

The fleet had arrived.

"Are you ready?" Soresh asked Luke.

"Ready for what?"

"Ready to fulfill your destiny, of course." He guided Luke over to a narrow gray console, just below the viewscreen. At its center was a glowing yellow button. "The resonance torpedoes are armed and ready to go," Soresh said. "Grand Moff Tarkin's greatest creation. One touch of this button will send them into the sun, kicking off a fusion chain reaction, and then . . ." He flung his arms in the air, blowing his lips out with the sound of an explosion. "If we hurry, we'll have time to watch the fireworks from space — before we navigate to safety, of course. I would never leave you behind, Luke," he said, as if Luke had expressed concern. "You're my ticket." He pulled something out of his cloak — the hilt of a lightsaber. "You'd like this back, wouldn't you?"

"If it pleases you," Luke said, trying to survey the room without moving his head. There were six guards, plus Soresh. If he had his lightsaber back and could find a blaster, there was a chance he could take down Soresh before the button got pressed. As long as he chose the exact moment to act.

Let the Force be your guide, the deep voice in his mind reminded him.

Soresh dangled the lightsaber before him. "You can have it back, for good," Soresh said. "All you need to do is press the button."

Luke didn't move.

"Now," Soresh urged him.

Now.

Luke struck out. His leg slashed across Soresh's knees, knocking the man to the floor. The lightsaber flew out of Soresh's hand and Luke snatched it out of midair.

"Kill him!" Soresh shouted.

The lightsaber blade lit up just as the guards started shooting. Luke slashed and hacked at the guards, but they evaded him. He was always a step behind, a moment too slow . . . maybe because now he understood those guards. He understood they were people just like him, doing what Soresh wanted them to do because they had no other choice. He didn't want to hurt them.

On the other hand, he didn't want to die.

Trying to remember his training, Luke swept the blade through the air, deflecting every laserbolt that came near him. Laserfire erupted in the room, scorching the walls and blasting through the giant computers. Exposed wiring sparked and soon flames licked at the walls. Foul, acrid black smoke choked the room, shrouding them in darkness. Laserfire streaked through the black, and Luke struck on instinct. Eyes squinted against the smoke, he had nothing but the Force to tell him where the next shot was coming from. Still, he wheeled on his feet, deflecting one shot after another, from all directions.

Soresh had dropped to the ground, and was slithering across the room on his belly. Luke felt the blade reaching toward him, as if the lightsaber wanted Soresh dead as much as Luke did. But the laserfire was backing him toward the far wall, and soon he was pinned. His blade was still blocking the shots, but his arms were tiring. He couldn't keep this up forever, and sooner or later his luck would run out. Even if it didn't, he would never be able to overpower Soresh. Not unless he could figure out a way to take out the guards — and there was no way he could defeat so many.

Especially since, from the sound of approaching footsteps, more were on the way. A wave of hopelessness washed over him, but Luke ignored it. There had to be *something* he could do, some way to defeat the enemy —

And then he got it. The guards weren't his enemies, he reminded himself. Not really. They were just men and women like him, except they hadn't had the strength to hold on. They'd lost themselves to Soresh. *He* was the enemy, of all of them. Luke just had to make them realize it. He continued to dart and weave away from the bolts of laserfire, as his mind worked feverishly, searching for a solution.

The Force can have a strong influence on the weak-minded, Ben had told him.

What could be weaker than a mind that was completely empty?

It was difficult to concentrate while he was swinging his lightsaber wildly and dodging laserbolts. But maybe that was better. Concentration had never helped his control of the Force. On the contrary, it was only when he *stopped* thinking, *stopped* trying that he ever succeeded. And so, without thinking about it anymore, or knowing what he was going to say, he spoke to the guards.

"You are someone!" he said.

"You do not belong to him!"

"He is not your master!"

He said the words with as much force as he could, again and again, trying to drown out the voice that was playing in their heads. But it wasn't working. The hail of laserfire continued to assault him in dangerous bursts. And somewhere, beneath the veil of smoke, he was sure he could hear Soresh laugh. At the sound, everything Soresh had done to him welled up in Luke and burst out of him.

"He is not our master," he said, pouring all his rage, all his pain, all his exhaustion, everything he was and had ever been into the words. "We do not belong to him."

Silence dropped over the room. A blaster clattered to the floor.

"Where am I?" someone mumbled.

"What am I doing?"

Sounds of confusion and fear — but no more explosions. No more laserfire. No more killing on command. It had worked — they were free.

Soresh's laughter cut through the noise. Luke whirled around. The Commander, bloody and shaken, but still on his feet, lunged toward the glowing yellow button. "Too late," Soresh said, and pressed the button.

Luke watched the viewscreen in horror as three resonance torpedoes hurtled toward the sun.

Luke leapt for the console, desperate to stop the torpedoes. There had to be some way of calling them back, or detonating them in midair, something to stop the inevitable. But there wasn't. And he'd wasted too much time searching — enough to give Soresh a head start on his escape. Luke took off after him, then hesitated in the doorway, torn. "You have to find a way off the planet!" he shouted at the confused guards. "If we stay here, we're all going to die!"

The confused buzzing in the room just got louder.

"Ships!" Luke shouted, frustrated. "We have to find ships!"

"Ships!" One of them cried, and took off running down the hall. Luke urged the rest to follow him. He had to help everyone off the planet, and he had to find a way to warn the Rebel fleet — and he had to catch Soresh. But he was only one man, and he couldn't do everything at once — so where was he supposed to start?

"Luke!" A familiar voice cried. A moment later, Leia appeared in the corridor, flanked by Han, Chewbacca, Ferus, and Div. The two droids wheeled behind them.

Luke's jaw dropped. "What are you doing here?"

"Rescuing you," Leia said, then spotted the fleeing guards. "Though it looks like you got tired of waiting."

Luke drew them back into the control room and explained everything that had happened. Chewbacca stayed in the corridor, guarding the door, while Ferus and R2-D2 took a long look at the launch controls. They both agreed: There was nothing they could do to stop the torpedoes. In less than three standard hours, the sun would explode. It would collapse into itself, generating a shock wave that would consume the entire star system. Nothing in its wake would survive.

Leia turned pale. "Half the fleet is up there!" she exclaimed. "We have to warn them."

C-3PO raised a golden hand. "With any prototype weapon of this sort, there is a one in three hundred twenty-seven chance that the weapon will fail."

Han snorted. "Normally, I'm all about playing the odds, but this game's a little too rich for my blood. What do you say we find the fleet and get out of here?"

"I fear that may be more difficult than it was a moment ago," Ferus said solemnly, his eyes fixed on the viewscreen behind their heads. The others turned around. Darth Vader's Interdictor Star Destroyer had just winked out of hyperspace. Six other Destroyers appeared a moment later. TIE fighters were already pouring out of them, firing on the Rebel ships.

"They were only expecting *two* Destroyers," Div said, alarmed. "And they thought there'd be time to lay an ambush. They can't handle this."

"And they can't flee the system when they're under this kind of fire," Han added.

For a brief moment they stood in silent horror, watching the battle unfold before them. Then Leia slammed a fist down on the launcher console with a loud crack. "They need help," she said, seizing control. "Luke, Han, Div — find ships. And the guards —"

"The guards won't be a problem," Luke told her.

"Then help them fight. I'll stay here and find some kind of communications equipment so I can fill in the fleet — and maybe I can get the Imperials to understand what we're dealing with."

"I'm not leaving you here alone," Luke said.

She glared at him. "I can take care of myself. The fleet can't."

"I'll stay with her," Ferus said quickly. "We have to evacuate this moon — there are still the hostages you told us about. We can't just leave them here to die."

"We're not leaving anyone here," Han said firmly. "You do what you need to do, Princess, then you make sure you get yourself off this rock. We're not leaving this system without you."

"Get up there, now," Leia ordered him, "or none of us will be leaving this system, period."

"As you wish, Your Worshipfulness," Han said. He grabbed Luke. "C'mon, kid, it's time for some target practice."

They rushed out of the room, hesitating only when Leia called after them, a note of panic in her voice. "Han! Luke!"

They turned back. She shot them another fierce glare. "Don't you *dare* get yourselves killed."

Leia watched with surprised respect as Ferus sorted through the mess of wires, stripping and splicing and finally rising in triumph. "We should be able to transmit now," he said.

She still couldn't believe this was the same Ferus Olin she'd known all those years on Alderaan. The same slimy, spineless suck-up she'd despised for most of her life. Of course, he'd gone by a different name then — but a new name wasn't supposed to change so much about a person. She was finally seeing the man her father had always promised her was there, behind Ferus's oily smile. The man who was brave and capable, who could be counted on. She just didn't understand why it had taken him so long to emerge.

War could make a hero out of almost anyone, she mused.

Just look at Han.

"Princess?" Ferus prompted her.

Leia shook off her thoughts. It was time for action. She contacted the fleet leader on a secure line and offered her authentication code.

"Princess Leia!" Commander Willard's voice came through the comm loud and clear. "What a relief you're safe."

"None of us are safe for much longer," Leia said quickly. "In two hours, twenty-seven minutes, this system's sun is going to explode."

"How can you possibly know—"

"It doesn't matter," Leia said. "The fleet will have to make the jump into hyperspace as soon as possible."

"Understood," Commander Willard said. "But we can't go anywhere under such heavy fire. We're putting everything we have into holding off the Imperials."

"Do what you can up there," Leia said. "And I'll do my best from down here."

"May the Force be with you, Princess."

"And you," Leia said, cutting the transmission. She'd never thought much about those words before meeting Luke. It was just something people said, calling on a meaningless superstition, just a habit or a lucky charm.

But since Luke had come into her life, she'd begun to understand that the Force was real. *If only it* were *with me*, she thought, not for the first time. *Imagine what I could do.* But there was no point in thinking about that. You fought with the weapons you had, not with the ones you wished for.

"Can you open a channel to the Imperial flagship?" she asked Ferus.

He nodded. "Do you think they'll listen to you?"

Not a chance. "It's worth a try," she said. Then she prepared herself. It was Vader's ship, which meant Vader himself might be on the other end of the line. The man she held responsible for the death of her home planet — and with it her father. *I will not lose control.*

But it wasn't Vader's distinctive voice. Just a faceless Imperial. Leia spoke without fear. "This is Princess Leia Organa of the Rebel Alliance," she said.

"What do you want, Rebel scum?" the Imperial spit out. "We'll accept nothing less than unconditional sur-render. Submit to us now, or die like the swine you are."

Now is not the time to fight, Leia reminded herself.

"This is not about our battle," she said, as calmly as possible. "This is about a common threat to us all."

"*Nothing* is a threat to the Empire," the Imperial said. "The sooner you learn that —"

Enough diplomacy. "The sun is about to explode,"

Leia said, her temper fraying. "Stop firing on the Rebel ships, get out of the system, and maybe you won't explode with it."

There was a sharp bark of laughter. "More pathetic Rebel tricks? When will you ever learn? The Empire is your destiny. Quit this ridiculous —"

Leia cut the line. "Either they'll analyze the solar spectrum and figure out I'm telling the truth, or they won't," she told Ferus. They needed to help the befuddled guards and the hostages find a way off the planet. Even if the Imperials kept fighting, at least some ships would be able to make it out of the system. "We can't afford to stand around and wait for them to decide to believe us."

"The fleet is strong, Princess," Ferus assured her. "And Div, Han, Luke . . . each of them will give everything to do defend the Rebellion. All they have."

Leia frowned, her eyes pinned on the viewscreen. It glowed with laserfire and explosions. "That's what I'm afraid of."

ire again, Chewie!" Han shouted into the comm. The Wookiee released another concussion missile. It screamed toward the nearest TIE fighter and collided with its cockpit. The Imperial ship exploded, unleashing a flakstorm. Han pulled up hard, straying right into a hail of laserfire.

"Whoa!" he shouted, as laserbolts strafed the hull. Sparks sprayed from the instrument panels and smoke plumed in the cockpit. "When I said fire, that's not what I meant," Han muttered, dropping into a sharp corkscrew to evade the Imperial ships.

A proton torpedo seared past, crashing into the X-wing on his starboard flank. Fractured and twisted pieces of durasteel and broken wings floated across the viewscreen. Ships were exploding on all sides of him. Laserfire blotted out the stars. All those weeks on the ground, Han had longed to be back in space again, behind the controls of his ship. But this wasn't exactly what he'd had in mind.

There had been twelve guards surrounding the *Falcon* — not exactly a challenge for the combined might of Luke, Han, Div, a Firespray, and an angry Wookiee. Han had been all ready to blast his way through, but Luke had stopped him in his tracks. "Let me deal with it," he'd said . . . and a moment later, the guards laid down their weapons. Han did his best not to look shocked, but Luke saw straight through it. "Jedi hokum," he'd explained with a laugh.

But after that, there was no more time for jokes or hokum. Div launched his Firespray, and Han and Chewbacca set off in the *Falcon*. Luke jumped into the X-wing he'd arrived with. They plunged into the thick of the battle, adding their firepower to the Rebel attack.

Han took out two more TIE fighters and then spotted Luke's X-wing zigzagging through the battlefield, three Imperials on his tail.

Han opened a comm link to the X-wing. "Luke, you've got company, six o'clock."

"I see them, but I can't shake them," Luke reported.

"Going in." Han reversed thrusters and swooped toward the TIE fighters chasing Luke. He pummeled them with laserfire, but they swerved out of reach. These guys were good.

Han was better. "On my mark, pull up, hard," Han told Luke.

"Copy that," Luke said, without question.

Han accelerated to full speed, dipping beneath the TIE fighters. "Now!" he shouted, and Luke's X-wing twisted in midair, shifting into a sharp climb. The TIE fighters overshot, and as they tried to compensate, Han picked them off one by one.

"Got 'em!" he crowed, grinning as the cockpit lit up with the glow of fiery wreckage. "You Imperial flyboys never learn, do —"

"Han!" Luke screamed through the comm link. "Pull up! Pull up, now!"

The *Millennium Falcon* was careening straight toward a squadron of TIE fighters. Their laser cannons were blasting at full force. Han yanked hard on the controls, but the ship didn't respond. The viewscreen showed smoke billowing from the port thrusters.

They were going to crash.

Luke didn't stop to think. He pivoted to his port side and swooped down toward the squadron of TIE fighters, strafing them with laserfire. Div's Firespray came in hard and fast from the other direction, spiraling and weaving in sync with Luke's maneuvering, as if they had coordinated the attack. The TIE fighters fanned out to evade the Rebel blasts. Div and Luke gave chase. The *Falcon* gave them cover as they zoomed through the maze of ships, firing without stop.

"Thanks for the save, kid." Han's voice came through the comm.

"What happened?" Luke asked. For a moment, he'd been sure the *Falcon* was going to crash straight into the Imperials.

"Little trouble with the nav system," Han said casually, as if he hadn't just narrowly avoided a fiery collision. "Nothing to worry about."

Luke shook his head and had to laugh. The *Falcon* didn't look like much of anything — except a pile of junk, that is. The *Millennium Falcon* was always breaking down — if it wasn't the particle shields, it was the hyperdrive or the aft sensory array — but Han always claimed the ship had never let him down, and never would. And Han was right about one thing: If you treated her right, she could fly like no ship Luke had ever seen.

Still, it was going to take more than a few good ships to untangle this mess. Luke never felt more at home than when he was behind the controls of a ship. He was able to clear his mind and focus it, all at once, letting himself become one with the machine. He dipped and glided, slipping through the web of Imperial attackers, watching his torpedoes streak through space. They always hit their mark.

But even if he shot down every ship he saw, he was only one pilot — there were hundreds of TIE fighters, maybe thousands of them. The Rebel fleet was barely holding its own.

The comm unit pinged. "You thinking what I'm thinking?" Div asked.

"We need to take out more ships," Luke said, stating the obvious.

"Not to mention stop from getting taken out ourselves," Han chimed in, as another X-wing burst into flame.

"Exactly," Div agreed. "And I've got an idea."

Luke listened as Div laid out his strategy. It was dangerous, and probably crazy.

Which meant it might actually work.

"On my mark!" Div barked into the comm. He pulled his ship into a whiplash turn. "Mark!" He looped up and around the squadron of TIE fighters, leading them on a wild chase through the battlefield. Han and Luke flanked him on either side, joined by several other Rebel ships. As planned, the Rebels didn't fire — they channeled all their power into the thrusters, narrowly outpacing the TIE pursuers.

"Faster," Div murmured, pushing the engines far past their breaking point. "Come on."

The cloud was nearly in reach. The Mon Calamari cruisers had done their part perfectly. The plasma bombs they'd detonated had expelled a massive cloud of gas.

It obscured a thousand meters of space behind an eerie red glow. The cloud would be harmless to ships passing through it, but was poison to navigational instruments, which meant as soon as they entered, they'd be flying blind. Perfect.

Div streaked into the cloud, letting his instincts guide the way, as they always had. He counted off the seconds aloud. "Three, two, one . . . Now!" he shouted into the comm. He yanked the controls, dropping the ship into a steep dive. Every Rebel ship did exactly the same. But the Imperials had no one to signal them — and no one to remind them that a Star Destroyer hovered on the other side of the cloud.

The squadron of TIE fighters slammed into the side of the ship, ripping a jagged hole in its hull. The massive ship began to list and shudder. Only a few of the TIE fighters peeled off in time, alerted by the explosions and shrapnel that danger lay ahead. Div wasn't about to give any of them a chance to shoot down the fleeing Rebels. As the X-wings followed orders and sped away, Div zoomed into the fray, picking off the TIE fighters one by one.

Dimly, through the comm, he heard Luke and Han urging some of the Rebel transport ships to activate hyperdrives while the Imperials struggled to regroup. The X-wings gave the larger ships cover, as they sped out of the system and winked into hyperspace. But Div's attention was laser-focused on the four ships that had survived the sneak attack, all of which were firing on him at once.

He was a good pilot.

The best.

But he couldn't evade missiles from four directions at once. One struck a glancing blow to his forward hull. Another blasted into his rear thrusters. Smoke filled the cabin. The navigational controls became sluggish . . . and then stopped responding altogether. Which meant whether he survived this encounter or not, he'd be of no use to the Rebel fleet. And since the hyperdrive had been blown out with the first missile, it was only a little longer before he'd be of no use to anyone.

But the laser cannons were still operational, and as the TIE fighters moved in for the kill, Div let them approach. "Just a little closer," he whispered. If this was going to be his last fight, he intended to win it.

They thought he was helpless, and were careless as they approached. Which gave Div one chance. He lined up the shot, then closed his eyes, waiting.

This time, he didn't have to try to connect to the Force. It was there for him, as Ferus had always promised him it would be. *Now.* He felt it, with a deep certainty. He pulled the trigger, and opened his eyes. A missile screamed into the nearest TIE fighter. The ship exploded, neatly splitting down the middle. Its solar energy collectors blew off in opposite directions, crashing into the two TIE fighters that flanked it. The fourth got caught in the blowback, and blew up a moment later.

Just not before it released one final torpedo.

Div had miscalculated — only slightly, but enough.

As the torpedo rocketed toward him, time seemed to slow. Unfortunately, it only gave him a chance to watch the end creeping closer.

He had chosen this sacrifice. It was probably a futile one, since all he'd done was buy the Rebels a bit more time.

But sometimes more time was all you needed.

The torpedo slammed into his ship and blew off his stabilizer fin. The ship spiraled out of control, spinning wildly in a cyclone of debris.

"Div!" Luke shouted through the comm.

"Make this count, Luke," Div said, but he suspected his communications system had failed, like the rest of them. Alarms were blaring through the ship as he plunged toward the moon's atmosphere.

There was nothing to do now but wait.

"Div!" Luke shouted again, but there was still no answer. The Firespray was bleeding exhaust and fuel as it dropped toward the moon. Within moments, it had slipped into the atmosphere. It sliced through the clouds, a red-hot ember growing dimmer and dimmer. And then it was gone. "We have to go after him," Luke cried.

"He's gone, kid," Han said. "But he bought us some time. Be grateful for that."

Luke knew he was right. The Rebels needed them up here, not down there, scouring the surface for wreckage.

And surely that's all there would be, wreckage. Even if Div had managed to eject before his ship burned up in the atmosphere, he could be stranded anywhere on the moon. That was millions of kilometers of ground to search — there was no way they could do that before the supernova. One way or another, Div was gone.

The fighting continued without him, but Han was right: Div had bought them some time. A good chunk of the fleet had managed to escape. Of course, that meant the ones that remained were more outnumbered than ever. Div wouldn't be the last to fall.

But Luke couldn't think about what might happen. He couldn't think about how narrow their chances were. He could only think about surviving each moment, and the next. The next TIE fighter, the next missile, the next laserbolt, the next explosion. The moments blurred and the battle seemed to stretch on forever, until Luke felt he'd been in this cockpit his entire life. He fired and fired again, and yet there were always new ships emerging from the wreckage. The Imperials would never give up.

And then the sky lit up with a bright, blinding flare.

First he thought another squadron had been taken

out, but this was brighter than a simple explosion, brighter than anything he'd ever seen. It seared his vision, and for a few seconds, he saw nothing but a glowing black.

He blinked hard, and gradually, the world came back. But it was a changed world: There was a roiling storm of fire where the dim sun had been. The resonance torpedoes had ignited their chain reaction — the sun began its collapse. The shock wave traveled at a small fraction of the speed of light, which meant they had a little time before it hit. About forty minutes, the droids had calculated — after that, the explosion would consume them all.

"This is Gold Leader," the voice came over the comm link. "The Imperials are fleeing. Repeat, the Imperials are fleeing. All ships return to base."

It was true. The firing had stopped, as understanding spread through both fleets. Star Destroyers and Rebel freighters alike were winking into hyperspace, desperate to flee the dying sun.

But Leia was still below, helping evacuate the moon. Which meant Luke wasn't going anywhere but down.

Y ou'll be fine," Ferus assured the stooped old woman, a streak of dried blood smeared across her face.

"Just activate the hyperdrive as soon as you're clear of the gravitational field," Leia instructed the pilot, as he climbed aboard the ship that Soresh had taken hostage one month before.

"Be brave for your mother," Ferus said, resting his hand on a young boy's scruffy brown hair. "She needs you."

One by one, the shaken settlers climbed aboard their ship. They had been trapped on the moon for weeks, locked inside dank cells with fading hope of escape. It seemed no one could believe that they were actually being given a ship, and a means to escape. But, weeping or smiling, they all climbed on board.

"That should be the last of them," Leia said.

Among the guards, confusion had proved contagious.

Without Soresh around to give them orders, they were easily swayed. With the help of the guards Luke had freed, Leia and Ferus had herded them all onto ships of their own. The moon was evacuated and sun would explode in thirty-eight minutes — which meant it was time for them to go.

After making one final sweep of the main base installation, Ferus and Leia retreated to the hangar, where the final ship of hostages was waiting for them.

It was the first time they'd really been alone together since Ferus had arrived on the moon. "I was very relieved to discover you were safe, Princess," Ferus told her. Leia would never know *how* relieved, just as she would never know that he had sworn his life to protect her. There was so much he hadn't told her — and so many lies that he had.

"I wasn't the one in real danger," Leia said, as they rushed toward the ship. "Luke was the one who risked everything. Sometimes I wonder . . ." She drifted off.

"Leia?" Ferus prompted her. It wasn't like the princess not to say exactly what was on her mind.

"I wonder what I would have done in his place," she admitted. "Whether I would have been strong enough to hold out against Soresh."

"Of course you would have!" Ferus assured her. "Princess, you're the strongest person I know."

But Leia shook her head. "But it isn't just strength, is it? Luke has something else . . . a certainty, a belief in his destiny. Even when everything else is stripped away, he still has . . ."

"The Force?" Ferus guessed.

Leia reddened, and a small laugh bubbled out of her. "I don't even know why I'm telling you this," she said. "It's ridiculous, I know. There's nothing Luke can do with his lightsaber that I can't do with my blaster. It's just sometimes I wonder how much more I could do for the Rebels, if I had his gifts. I wonder if I could have saved —" She stopped, abruptly.

But Ferus knew what she was thinking. "What happened to Alderaan is not your fault, Princess. You couldn't have stopped it."

"You're right," Leia said, looking away. "*I* couldn't."

Ferus was quiet for a moment. He listened to the sound of their pounding footsteps. Then he made a decision. "Leia, stop," he said, and grabbed her arm.

"We've got less than half an hour," Leia said. "That doesn't leave much time for sightseeing."

"Just a second," Ferus said. "Indulge an old man."

She stopped running, and gave him an impatient stare. "Well, what is it?"

She took his breath away, this fierce, brave woman she had become. When he looked at her, he still saw the inquisitive toddler, the willful child, the rebellious teenager — he saw her entire life, and understood it had all led up to this moment. She was ready.

Ready to know the truth — ready to know her destiny.

No longer would he allow her to live in ignorance. No longer would he let her feel powerless or *less than*. No longer could he stand hearing her question her own strength. No longer would he listen as she doubted herself.

Obi-Wan had tried so hard to convince him it was better this way. That Luke would be their warrior and Leia their spare, their backup, in case anything went wrong. Obi-Wan believed that Luke would be the galaxy's savior, that the risk of hiding the truth would pay off. But Obi-Wan also believed that Ferus should trust his instincts.

And his instincts were telling him that Luke and Leia would be stronger together. That the Force lived within her, and she deserved the chance to know it, to know herself — and to know her brother.

"There's something I haven't told you," he said, aware that after this moment, nothing would be the same. "Something you need to know."

"What is it?" she asked impatiently. "We have to leave."

"Leia, I—" Suddenly, he couldn't catch his breath. His lungs squeezed together as if trapped in a vise. A curtain of darkness descended across his vision. It was as if the air had turned to poison, killing him with every breath.

And, as he reached out with the Force, he heard it, the breathing, heavy and even, wheezing death with every exhalation.

Vader was here.

And he was close.

"I heard something," he said quickly. "Back in the base. Belowground." They were at the mouth of the hangar. "It sounded like a cry for help. I think there might be more prisoners."

"I don't hear anything," Leia said. "And time's running out. Are you sure?"

"I'm sure," Ferus said urgently. He had to get her out of here before Vader got close enough to sense her presence. They'd met face-to-face before, and Ferus couldn't believe that Vader hadn't figured out the truth. There was no way he was going to risk giving Vader another chance again. Because even if he didn't realize who Leia was, he would surely take her prisoner — or kill her.

"Then we have to go back and help them," Leia said.

"I'll go," Ferus said. He would do whatever it took to stall Vader and give Leia time to escape. It was the only way to make sure she survived.

"I'm not letting you go on your own!" Leia said, indignant.

There was little time to argue. "Leia, please," Ferus said. "I promised your father I would protect you. Don't make me break that promise. If there's anyone back there, I'll help them. I'll be fine. Please — just go."

He could tell it was the last thing she wanted to do. But maybe she saw his desperation.

"All right," she finally said. "But if your ship doesn't take off in ten minutes, I'm coming back for you."

Ferus grasped her hands and gave them a tight squeeze — it was as much of a good-bye as he could allow himself. If she knew what he was about to do — and how it would most likely end — she would never let him go.

Leia boarded the freighter and Ferus ran into the base, back the way they'd come. Back toward Vader. He didn't have far to run. As he rounded one corner, and then another, the stench of evil grew overwhelming, the air thick with darkness. And then, just beyond the second corner, there he was. Darth Vader, standing still in the middle of the hall, as if he were waiting. As if he knew exactly what was coming, and who.

Ferus froze at the opposite end of the corridor. He couldn't force his legs to carry him any closer.

"I had hoped you were dead," Darth Vader said in a low rumble.

"Sorry to disappoint you." Rage swelled within Ferus. He hadn't come face-to-face with Vader since that day, so many years ago, when the Sith had left him for dead. When Ferus had failed to avenge Roan's death, and left Vader alive, to kill so many more. Because Ferus failed, Vader lived to strike down Obi-Wan. To destroy nearly everything and everyone he touched. Standing before him, Ferus understood the true nature of hate.

He had told himself that he only wanted to stall Vader, to protect Leia. But that wasn't the whole truth.

He wanted another chance at killing the Dark Lord. He wanted to stand over Vader's body and watch him die.

"I could kill you where you stand," Vader said. "I could kill you with a thought."

"It would probably be easier," Ferus replied lightly. He knew he had to leave behind his hatred if he was going to survive this encounter. He couldn't beat Vader by matching him darkness for darkness. His rage would only cloud his connection to the Force; he needed to stay clear. "And you always were one to take the easy way out. *Anakin.*"

"Anakin is dead," Vader said.

"So you've told me before," Ferus said. "You killed him. Just like you killed Obi-Wan. And Padmé." He watched carefully, hoping for some flinch, some sign, *something* to indicate that the name had some impact. If Anakin really was dead and gone, then Ferus had no chance left at all. Perhaps none of them did. "Erase all reminders of who you used to be, isn't that the plan? Any reminders of what you've done and how much it hurts?"

"You know nothing about pain," Vader said. Then he raised his lightsaber. The red beam glowed in the darkness. "But it will be my pleasure to teach you."

Darth Vader had come for Luke Skywalker. He had come to find the boy who had caused so much trouble, wrought so much destruction — and somehow, inexplicably, bore Anakin's name.

But he had stayed — even when it became clear that Luke was gone, along with everyone else — because he sensed there was someone else hiding in the bowels of the station. Someone *familiar*. A presence that evoked strange and unsettling images of the past, of things he hadn't thought about for many years. Images of *Padmé* — her scent, the soft melody of her voice, the myriad details he'd spent two decades trying to forget. It meant there was someone on this station connected to his past, and that someone needed to die.

As he swept through the halls, he had been almost . . . not afraid, certainly. Fear was beneath him now, useful only as a weapon with which to destroy his enemies.

No, he had been *watchful*, wondering who he might find lurking around the next corner.

Discovering Ferus had been a relief. This was no unknown variable from the past. Ferus was known, easily dealt with. A loose end he should have tied up long before. Ferus had no power over him; his words were empty. He was nothing but a feeble old man babbling about a dead past. And yet the sight of him — the sound of the name *Padmé* on his lips — was enraging. Ferus should be dead, as all the Jedi should be dead. It was infuriating that he was still crawling around like a Bossuk roach.

No longer. Vader stoked the rage, let it swell within him. His rage was his power — something the pathetic Jedi had never understood. His rage was bottomless; his power was limitless.

Ferus was nothing in the face of that. Less than nothing. A roach, to be squashed underfoot.

Vader crossed the distance between them before the old man even had time to draw his weapon. *I could kill him with a single blow*, Vader thought. But there was no hurry. And he had to admit, he was curious. Ferus had become such a decrepit human specimen, paunchy and sad. *Soft*. It would be interesting to let him believe he could still put up a fight.

Vader swung his blade down. Ferus met it solidly. There was a dull hum as the red and blue blades clashed.

"Your technique has become lazy," Vader observed. He parried a blow, almost as an afterthought.

Ferus didn't reply. He was breathing heavily, gasping with each lunge and thrust. Vader deflected every strike with little more than a flick of the wrist.

"And you've gotten complacent," Ferus said, slashing diagonally. Vader retreated a step, and the lightsaber hummed through empty air. "You think no one can match you, right? Same old Anakin."

"Anakin is *dead*!" Vader roared, and struck with his full power. Time to end this game.

But Ferus somehow evaded the blow — and then danced away from the next one, and the next. The blue blade whirled and spiraled through the air, matching Vader strike for strike, blow for blow.

It was that *name*. That was the only explanation. Even the sound of it had somehow thrown him off balance.

This was unacceptable.

"You move well for a fat old man," Vader granted. He was more powerful by far, but the plastoid armor made for awkward maneuvering. And he would never reclaim the physical grace he'd had as Anakin.

Vader shook off the thought, disgusted with himself. Anakin had nothing that he wanted, *nothing*. He let the disgust grow. *This* was what he needed. Not grace, not that foul Jedi concentration. Anger.

Darkness. Control.

Ferus leapt through the air, driving the lightsaber down in a chopping motion as he arced toward the ground. The blade came within centimeters of Vader's face plate. Sweat poured down Ferus's face with the effort of continuing the fight. And yet still, he lived. "No older than you, Anakin," he gasped.

And it was true. They'd once been the same age, young and stupid, easily manipulated by their Jedi Masters. Now *Vader* was Master of all — and Ferus was this weak, stooped thing. Is this what Anakin would have grown into, had he stayed in that frail, human body? This sagging bag of loose flesh?

Vader was furious with himself for entertaining the thought. It didn't matter what Anakin would have become. Anakin was nothing — didn't exist, had never existed.

"There is no Anakin," Vader said,

"And yet here he is in front of me," Ferus countered. "The same cocky, deceitful, defiant, *scared little boy* you always were. You killed Obi-Wan because he saw the fear behind the mask. You killed Padmé because she saw the monster."

Rage blotted out Vader's vision, turning the world to darkness — everything disappeared but Ferus's disgusting, knowing smile. Ferus was the one who had never changed, was still the same insufferable child he'd always been. Vader should have done the galaxy a favor and snuffed him out at the Academy. Better late than never.

Ferus advanced with a dizzying series of strikes and parries. "You can kill me, if you want. But you will never kill Anakin. I suspect someday, he'll kill you."

"Someday, perhaps." Vader flicked a gloved hand, and Ferus's lightsaber flew across the hall. "But unfortunately for you, that day is not today." He plunged his blade through Ferus's heart, and watched with pleasure as Anakin's long-lasting enemy dropped to the ground, the life draining from his eyes.

The pathetic old man knew nothing, he told himself. Anakin was dead and gone forever. And now there was no one who could bring him back.

Ferus lay still, as the thundering footsteps disappeared down the corridor. He lay on his back in a pool of blood, feeling his life force trickle away. And he lay with a smile on his face, knowing that he had succeeded.

He would have liked to kill Darth Vader.

He would have liked to save the galaxy.

But it was enough to know he had saved Leia.

He had always thought dying would hurt. But there was little pain. There was little of anything, anymore. The bonds holding him to this world were fraying.

"Be brave, my friend. You have done well." Obi-Wan knelt beside him. Not the glowing, translucent spirit Ferus had come to know, but the real Obi-Wan, solid as he had been when he was alive. The Jedi Master took Ferus's hand. "The end is never the end," he said. "Only another journey."

More riddles, Ferus thought wryly. Leave it to Obi-Wan to be frustratingly vague, even at a time like this. He would have laughed, but he lacked the strength. Obi-Wan smiled, as if he knew.

And then Obi-Wan faded away, and another figure appeared in his place.

Ferus gasped, choking on the blood that bubbled in his throat. His lips formed the name he hadn't spoken aloud in years.

Soft fingers brushed his forehead. "Did you really think I would leave you here alone?"

You left me alone for all those years, Ferus wanted to say. *I always hoped you were waiting for me. I always hoped I would see you again.*

Roan Lands, dead for nearly two decades, gazed down at him, his eyes full of warmth and humor. Roan, who had found Ferus after he'd fled the Jedi Temple, and taught him what it meant to truly live. Roan, who had been Ferus's partner and friend for the best years of his life. Roan, whom he thought he'd lost forever.

Ferus's fear was gone, replaced by a deep, calming peace. He had done what he could for the people he loved. He had fulfilled the mission Obi-Wan had set out for him, protected Anakin's child until she was strong enough to protect herself. He had fought as best he knew how, for as long as he could. And now Roan was here, and Ferus was ready to go.

"I'll stay with you," Roan said, squeezing his hand. "For as long as you need me."

Ferus let his eyes drift shut. His world narrowed to the sound of Roan's voice, and the warmth of Roan's hand.

"You are not alone," he heard Roan say.

And then he heard nothing at all.

"You are not alone," Leia whispered, squeezing Ferus's hand even tighter, wishing she could give him her strength.

But she couldn't.

All she could do was kneel by his body and watch as his chest rose and fell with slow, shallow breaths . . . and then fell still. There was a faint smile on his face, and Leia hoped it meant he had died in peace.

He was dead.

Leia had known Ferus all her life, but she felt she'd only *really* known him these last few months. She felt a hole open within her, as if she'd lost a part of her family, or even herself. He was the last connection she'd had to her past on Alderaan, and to her father. It always seemed like he had secrets he was desperate to share with her, if only she'd asked the right questions. But she'd never bothered to ask.

And now he was gone.

If she'd come back for him sooner, maybe she could have stopped it — whatever, whoever it was that had done this to him.

Leia knew she had to go. The sun was about to explode. And whoever had killed Ferus might still be here — might be coming back for her.

But she didn't move. She stayed by his side, holding his hand. *Just a little longer*, she told herself, *and then I'll go.*

She didn't want to leave him alone.

eia!" Luke finally spotted the princess, kneeling beside what looked like a body. He hurried over to her, Han following close behind. Luke had a bad feeling as he approached the body, but forced himself to look at the man's face. "What happened to him?"

Leia just shook her head.

Luke hadn't known Ferus very long or very well, but there had been something about the man that seemed so familiar, something that made him feel like part of the family. A family that was very quickly dying off.

"How about we move this party to the ship," Han said. "Before we get toasted."

Leia shot him a quick, wounded look, and he immediately softened his tone. "I'm sorry, Princess," he said quietly. "But we have to go."

"I know," she admitted, and released Ferus's hand. "I hate to leave him."

Luke cleared his throat. "We won't."

He shared a glance with Han, and they both bent down on either side of Leia to raise the body of the fallen Jedi.

Leia took hold of Ferus' hand once again. "Let's go."

They walked in silence toward the edge of the camp where the *Falcon* was docked. Chewbacca had kept the engines running. The entire fleet had jumped into hyperspace, along with the Imperials. They were the only ones left in the system, with six minutes to go. But just as they were about to take off, Luke froze.

"What is it, kid?" Han asked impatiently.

Luke raised a pair of microbinoculars to his eyes. More than a kilometer away, a figure in a black robe swept toward an Imperial shuttle.

"Vader," Luke said darkly. "You think he . . ."

"Yes," Leia said, without doubt. "He killed Ferus."

Luke activated his lightsaber. "And I'm not letting him get away with it."

"Luke, there's no time," Leia said.

"And there's no way you face him and live," Han added.

Luke didn't care. He was tired of running from Vader. It was time to face the enemy head on. After everything he'd been through, hadn't he proven his strength? He felt like he could do anything — and right now, destroying Vader was the only thing he wanted to do. Leia grabbed his arm.

"Luke, *think*. He'll kill you, you know that. And even if he doesn't, even if by some miracle, you manage to defeat him, it'll be too late to escape. You'll die in the shock wave." The enormous sun loomed overhead, blotting out much of the sky.

"Then either way, Vader will die," Luke said. "All I have to do is stall him, keep him from boarding that shuttle, and he's gone forever. Isn't that worth the sacrifice?"

Han snorted. "Sacrifice is overrated."

"He doesn't understand," Luke said to Leia. "But you must. After everything he's taken from you —"

"I won't let him take you, too!" Leia shouted, as close to losing control as he had ever seen her. She grabbed him by both shoulders. "How many people have given their lives so you could survive?" she asked him. "You think you can throw your life away, like it's *nothing*?"

Luke gritted his teeth. "It'd be worth it."

"Nothing's worth that," Han argued. "We'll have another chance. And when the time comes, we'll be there. We'll have your back."

"The galaxy needs you," Leia said. "We need you. And *you need us*."

Luke had learned something from his imprisonment: No matter how many friends you have, no matter how determined they are to remain by your side, some things have to be faced alone. Sometimes you only had your own strength to draw from; you only had yourself to rely on.

And something told Luke that the day he finally faced Darth Vader would be one of those times.

But not yet.

Not today.

Luke watched the black-robed figure getting smaller and smaller as he swept toward his ship. *I will watch you die*, he thought. *I will make you pay for everything you've done.*

But today, instead of taking Vader's life, he would save his own. "Let's get out of here," he said, and began climbing into the *Falcon*. Leia and Han stood in the hatchway, watching him board. Suddenly, Leia's eyes widened. "Behind you!" she cried.

Luke whirled around, fumbling for a weapon. A bloodied and ragged Soresh stood at the base of the ship.

"Did you really think I would let you leave this moon alive, Luke?" Soresh shouted up at him. "You will always belong to me!" Soresh raised a blaster — just as a bolt of laserfire hit him squarely in the chest.

He toppled to the ground.

"See what I mean, kid?" Han asked. He slipped his blaster back into its holster and grinned. "That's another one you owe me."

The shock wave blasted through the star system, steamrolling everything in its path. A small, dead moon was no match for its explosive power. The storm of fire and radiation overwhelmed the moon, blasting it to dust and ash. Within seconds, the moon was gone. Only glowing radiation and swirling debris were left behind. And still, the supernova's thirst was unquenched. The shock wave rolled on, killing one planet after another. Until what had been a star system was nothing more than a blinding glow, stretching across billions of kilometers of space.

It almost looked alive, pulsing and expanding, constantly reborn.

But looks were deceiving; it wasn't a life. It was a long and fiery death. For the sun, for the system — and for any living creature foolish enough to be caught in its wake.

"There it goes," Luke said, as the white dot on the viewscreen swelled into a luminous smear, brighter than a galaxy. Hard to believe that he was watching the death of an entire star system.

Harder still to believe that Ferus and Div were lost in the inferno, and would never be seen again.

"You think Vader made it out in time?" Leia asked. They'd left the moon with only minutes to spare and fled the system without looking back.

"He was cutting it close," Han pointed out. "Maybe Soresh did us all a favor and toasted the guy once and for all."

Luke shook his head. It was a nice dream, but he knew better. "He's still out there," Luke said. "I can feel it."

There was a tense silence. Then Han cleared his throat. "You know what we all need?"

"Sleep," Luke said. He suddenly realized how exhausted he was, emotionally and physically. This was the first time in a long time he'd had a chance to think — and he didn't like the thoughts that were crowding into his head. "I'll be in my bunk," he said, standing up. "I need to be alone for a while."

"That's the last thing you need," Han insisted. "Follow me."

Luke was too tired to argue. He waited as Han set the ship to autopilot, then followed him and the rest of his friends to the main hold.

"You, too, grease buckets," Han told the droids, when they hesitated. "Consider it an order."

Everyone settled around the large table in the middle of the main hold, and Han poured them all glasses of lum. Then Han raised his own glass. "To absent friends," he said. "Their sacrifices won't be forgotten."

"I thought you didn't believe in sacrifice," Leia teased him.

"I believe in getting the job done," Han said. "So did Div."

"And Ferus," Leia added, quietly.

Chewbacca roared, giving Han a hearty thump on the back.

"When you're right, you're right, buddy," Han said. He raised the glass higher. "Okay, to absent friends — and present ones." He glanced at the droids, then at Leia. "No matter how annoying they may be."

"To annoying friends," Leia repeated, holding his gaze.

As they clinked their glasses together, the room bubbled with laughter and conversation. Luke leaned back in his chair and let the sounds of friendship wash over him, thinking about how much he'd lost — and how much he still had left. He wondered how long they had before the next crisis, the next battle, the next loss. Because as long as there was an Empire, and a dark side, these moments of peace could never last. There would always be another fight. But one day, Luke promised himself, there would be one final fight — and one final victory.

Luke could only hope that when the day came, he and his friends would face it together.

TWO YEARS LATER

The world was white. Snowflakes swirled in gusts of icy wind. The ground lay buried far beneath a thick layer of snow and ice. As the sun dropped beneath the horizon, the temperature dropped well below freezing. By day, the planet Hoth was only barely habitable; at night, it was a dead zone. There was no shelter from the snow, no refuge from the raking winds. It seemed impossible anything could survive such wintry torment. And yet, two creatures stumbled blindly through the frozen landscape.

One rode a tauntaun, prodding the weary animal to take one more step, and yet another, and another. The cold bit into him with sharp teeth, but he pushed on, scanning the horizon for any sign of life.

Several kilometers of snow and ice lay between him and what he sought. A lone man, crawling through the snow, losing strength by the second. Soon his limbs grew too numb to move, and he collapsed, facedown in the snow.

A third figure watched them both. A figure unbowed by the wind. A figure that was draped only in a thin, brown robe, and yet did not feel the cold.

He had been watching for a long time, watching and waiting.

But now, that time had ended.

The time for action was upon him.

Han Solo was steering his tauntaun the wrong way. If he continued on his course, he would lose himself in the blizzard and never find his way back to Echo Base. While Luke would lie helpless in the snow, growing weaker and weaker, until he finally succumbed to the cold.

Obi-Wan reached out with the Force. Using the Force was different now, beyond the grave. He was stronger and weaker at the same time. In many ways, he *was* the Force. It animated his spirit, gave him this strange half-life — but it also separated him from the living world. He couldn't save Luke himself. But he could help Han.

Just a few degrees to the east, and a bit to the south, and Han would be on a direct course to his friend. It was little more than a gentle nudge in the right direction. Han trusted his instincts — Obi-Wan was only giving those instincts a bit of help. Whether Han would be able to keep Luke alive and get him back to the base, Obi-Wan couldn't know. But he had faith in both of them. He'd never seen such strong wills to survive.

It was time. Han would find Luke soon, and before he did, there was something Obi-Wan needed to say.

"Luke," Obi-Wan said, materializing before him.

There was no response. Had he waited too long?

"Luke," he said again, louder.

Luke raised his head. "Ben?" he asked weakly, his eyes widening.

There was so much Obi-Wan would have liked to say, but there was little time. "You will go to the Dagobah system," he said.

"Dagobah system?" Luke sounded confused. It was not surprising. Very few humans had ever heard of Dagobah — it was one of the reasons Yoda had stayed safely hidden for so long.

"There you will learn from Yoda, the Jedi Master who instructed me."

Luke didn't understand, but he soon would. Obi-Wan had no doubt the young Jedi would follow his instructions and find his way to Dagobah — and there he would find Yoda, and his training could finally begin. Obi-Wan had watched the boy for three years, waiting to be *sure* that he was strong enough to learn the Jedi way. That he wouldn't be tempted to the dark side. That he was not another Anakin. Obi-Wan knew he shouldn't blame himself for the rise of the Empire — the rise of darkness — but he still bore the guilt.

He refused to release another such evil on the galaxy.

And so he had waited, and waited, desperate to be sure.

But he had finally come to accept: You could never be sure.

You could only hope; you could only believe. He had come to know Luke well these past years, and he knew that Luke was no Anakin. He was his own man, strong enough to take on the burden and gift of being a Jedi. The training would be difficult, and there would be many temptations along the way. Luke would hear the call of the dark side . . . but Obi-Wan believed the boy would resist. And once Yoda had the chance to know Luke, Obi-Wan was sure he would agree.

Trust your instincts. Trust the Force. Words he had learned from his Masters, repeated to so many Padawan, to so many fallen friends.

He was finally ready to follow his own advice.

As Han Solo appeared on the horizon, Obi-Wan allowed himself to fade away. It was only a matter of time now. Luke would survive to fly to Dagobah. He would train. He would learn. Soon, he would be ready. The Jedi would return. And the fight for the galaxy could truly begin.